The Real Me Because of You

M.J. Apple

Copyright © 2022 Creative Reflections Media

This is a work of fiction. Names, characters, businesses, events, and incidents are the products of the author's imagination. Any resemblance to actual persons, living or dead, or actual events is purely coincidental.

All rights reserved. No part of this book may be reproduced or used in any manner without the written permission of the copyright owner except for the use of quotations in a book review.

SECOND EDITION

Kindle	Paperback	Hardcover
ASIN : B0BQGM2K7K	ASIN : B0BMDH8XBH	ASIN : B0BN5PP41W
	ISBN : 9798363805912	ISBN : 9798364176943

Book Design Cover: Veronica Jimenez

To my husband.

I'm blessed to have someone who puts up with my neurotic mentality.

Thank you and I love you!

PROLOGUE

The weekly family dinner. Yes, that's still a thing in my family. Usually, I can get out of it, living two hours away and working as a teacher. But somehow, my sister and mom guilt me into driving up before the beginning of the fall semester.

"Anak[1]," my Filipina mother informs me that my cousin is joining us. "Your pinsan[2] Enrico is bringing David. You can work on your classroom next week. I don't know how much longer you'll have me…."

I know perfectly well that she is in good physical health but still tries to pull me in. I want to say no, knowing that all I will hear is judgment and criticism while my older sister and her perfect family get all the praise and glory.

"We will make halo-halo[3]," she insists, knowing my fondness… or weakness, in this case, is sweets, and nothing can beat that delicious Filipino specialty.

• • •

However, as food is served in the formal dining room, I immediately wish I didn't make this drive. My eight-year-old niece is reciting Roosevelt's epic fireside chat, no doubt

---

[1] Filipino translation: child

[2] Filipino translation: cousin

[3] An icy Filipino dessert with various toppings/treats. Literal translation is mix-mix.

encouraged by Ate[4] Angela, her ever-doting mother, and my overachieving sister, while her five-year-old twin siblings run amok around the table.

Ricky, our younger cousin, groans as our nephew grabs an adobo[5] drumstick off his plate. "Ate," he attempts to grab Angela's attention. She gives him a dirty look as if he's interrupting Katie's little presentation. "Could you *please* control your children?" He points to the little boy with his lips and motions that this is David's, Ricky's newest beau, first time meeting any member of our family.

Of course, our mother chooses that exact moment to bring out more food from the kitchen. "Oh, Enrico, they are young. David, have more food."

"It's okay, Mrs. Macayo," David attempts to decline, but she is already ladling more adobo onto his plate. He looks to Ricky for help, but Ricky is still trying to get his drumstick away from Archie.

Katie finishes her little soliloquy by this time, and our mother ceremoniously puts the serving dish down to clap her hands enthusiastically. "She is reading at a middle school level," Angela brags proudly. "I may have Isa pull some strings to get her to Wellingworth early." She looks at me.

---

[4] A Filipino title for older sister or female cousin

[5] A simple saucy Filipino dish featuring chicken or pork, usually served over rice

"You want a little kid at a boarding school full of horny teenagers?" Ricky guffaws.

"Are you the admissions director there?" David inquires.

Before I can respond, our mother answers. "She's a teacher," our mother states evenly. "She could've been an engineer or something more… ano ang salita[6]?" She asks my sister and cousin for English words to describe what she feels is a better career choice for me.

"Prestigious?" Angela offers.

"Profitable?" Ricky quips.

"Prominent?" David adds.

The eldest Filipina sighs. "Yes, yes…. instead she act and get no jobs, she teach… Why can't you go into medicine like your Ate?"

I lower my head and pick at my food. This dinner couldn't finish sooner.

---

[6] Filipino translation: How do you say?

CHAPTER 1

I return to town shortly before 9:00 pm, parking in the lot behind my building, and my best friend, Amelia Cartwright, is waiting at the back door with a bottle of wine.

"No leftover containers?" she asks brightly as I unlock the door and start on the first of two flights to my third-floor flat.

"I declined." I finally have the opportunity to speak for myself again.

"Declined?"

"Okay, more like left without grabbing the food," I elaborate. Mia knows me too well, including how I can't stand up to my family. I stop at the top of the first flight and stare at one of the second-floor apartment door, which was ajar.

"Earth to Isa." Mia nudges me, and when I still don't move, she goes around me. She looks in the same general direction. "What are we looking at?"

"The door is open."

She gives me a perplexed look. "Yes, that's what doors do. They open. They close."

"No one lives there."

We look in silence for a moment. "Well, the Fritzes don't have to let you know if they let the place out." She grins, hands me the bottle of wine, and heads toward the dark apartment.

"What are you doing?" I ask, knowing full well what the answer is. She's always been the risk taker, the one whose curiosity led her to trouble and love. That's why she's happily living with her long-time boyfriend Wesley, and I'm destined to be a spinster.

She glances briefly at me and enters. I nervously shift my weight from one foot to the other and peek at the only other apartment door on this floor. Old Joe Rivera is probably asleep right now. I sigh and follow my best friend through the door.

My eyes adjust to the darkness of the place, my senses on full alert. Who knows what is in here? Cobwebs? Cockroaches? A corpse? That last thought lingers on my mind, what if someone's dead body is in here, and our fingerprints make us the prime suspects?

"Mi -" Her name begins to come out of my mouth when something touches me. I scream and run out of the apartment. Mia follows me out, laughing hysterically.

The other apartment door swings open, and Old Joe exits with a bat. His stance is ready for battle. He looks around and sees us. He scowls. "Luisa!"

"I'm sorry, Joe," I am still trembling.

"It is Sunday night and very late. Don't you have to teach tomorrow?" He turns to Mia. "Don't you have a job to go to?"

"Yessir," Mia salutes in jest. "Text me later," she whispers as she runs downstairs, still giggling.

"You are grown, women. Not teenagers… hell, you're closer to thirty," Old Joe exhales. 32, I remind myself silently. "You need to act your age. Get a husband. Make a family. And stop these childish games."

"I'm sorry," I repeat.

He looks at the door to the other apartment. "Gerald was showing that today. We may get a new neighbor soon." He walks over there and closes the door before heading to his abode.

I stand in an empty hallway, looking at the closed door, imagining who could be moving in below me.

CHAPTER 2

I roll over with the sun peeking through my blinds and look at my clock, 7:38. I groan, thinking this is my last day or two of sleeping in as students move into the dorms on Thursday. While I enjoy my job, I cherish sleep as they are sometimes far and few in between during the school year, especially during theater production times. Even though I teach math (the only available position when I got my teaching certification), I am often tapped to be the assistant director of the productions due to my knowledge of the art.

As I prepare for the day, I see an email I must have missed from yesterday. Jane Tromberg informs me that I have a meeting with the headmaster at 9:00 am. I look at the time, 8:04. Shoot…. I don't have time for a full-blown shower and primping or my contacts. I brush my teeth, put my hair in a ponytail, and don a nice t-shirt and jeans. I run out the door and am delayed on the second floor with two people moving in a couch into the empty apartment. I briefly make eye contact with one of the movers, the cute one who is closer to landing. He smiles. His smile and face seem familiar, but I couldn't place it as I focus on getting out there.

"Sorry, love," he says with a slight accent. British, I think, mixed with a midwestern cadence. "Hey, Colin, can we move a little faster?" I hear a grunt from inside the apartment in response.

They allow me to squeeze by, and I brush against the man's forearm as I pass. "Thanks," I mumble as I speed down the stairs and into my car. As I take the short drive to the school, I attempt to think what this meeting may be about but instead think about the handsome man who was moving into the apartment or helping his friend Colin move into the apartment. I'm hoping it's the first idea.

I run into the main office lobby with a minute or two to spare. Jane Tromberg, the headmaster's longtime administrative assistant, is sitting at her usual perch, preparing for the upcoming school year. Looking around, I don't think it has changed much since I was a student, and much of the mainstay furniture is still in the same places. The chairs, the computer and the phone system have all been updated, but it's still all very familiar.

Jane looks up from her screen with a smile. "Ah, Luisa! I'm glad you made it. I wasn't sure you got my message. I was about to call you to confirm, but as you can see," she nods at all the things on her desk, "we're all quite bogged down." I gave her an understanding nod. "Are you prepared for the year to begin? I cannot believe that the fall semester is here again. It seems like graduation was just yesterday." I adjust my glasses with my index finger and smile as she reminisces.

She types a few things on her computer. "Tell me," she asks with a smile, "how was your summer? Did you do anything interesting? Meet new people?" Her question pertains to having a significant other; being the only single female teacher, the other ladies attempt to play matchmaker with me, except I don't take their bait. It's not that I don't want to be alone for the rest of my life, but it's just I don't want to feel that pain and rejection again.

I give her a small smile. "I spent a lot of time in Stonehaven, helping with their arts center's theatre group and camps."

She tuts. "You're not a spring chicken anymore, dear. You need to start hunkering down and start a family."

The door to the office opens, and Dr. Andreas Teague appears. This elderly gentleman has been a cornerstone to this school… heck, this community for as long as I can recall. He has a grandfather-type personality but can also be stern when it comes to discipline. "Miss Tromberg," he says with a jovial tone. "You aren't roping Miss Macayo into dating one of your grandchildren's friends, are you?"

She sighs. "No…"

He stands aside and ushers me to his office. "But she would if she could," he adds as I enter. I stifle a laugh because truer words have never been spoken. The older man gestures toward several comfortable chairs on one side of the room, and I take one of them.

"Coffee?" He goes to the nook that has a small bar.

Realizing I haven't had breakfast or a chance to stop by the cafe, I acquiesce. "Yes, please. Cream and sugar?"

After a moment, he hands me a cup. "I know it's not as good as the coffee shop in town…" I take a sip and sigh.

"It's okay, Doctor. I brew my own instead of going downstairs often. It can get pretty expensive after a while." I take another sip.

Dr. Teague laughs. "You were always the realist, Miss Macayo."

"Really?" My mom would have said Angela and then comment how I spent too much money going to college and have nothing to show for it. As it is, I'm back in my alma mater teaching a subject I am only mildly interested in instead of doing something more productive with my life.

"Absolutely. Just because you're a realist doesn't mean you can't be a dreamer too. Maybe your dreams are just another part of the reality that you're living."

I blink. What?

The headmaster laughs again. "You are a great actress, young lady, and we are truly grateful that you are sharing your gift with the future thespians."

So why can't I get a job acting?

Dr. Teague takes a sip from his cup. "That's part of the reason why I called you in this morning." I wait for a second, waiting for him to continue. "There's an opening in the English department, and I wanted to allow you to take the position."

I look at him. "Who isn't coming back?"

"Georgette Stein is no longer with us."

I gasp. Georgette Stein is… was?… in charge of the drama department. She is the glue that held the productions together. She coordinates, produces, directs… basically controls the whole thing. "What… what happened to her?"

He chuckles. "My apologies, Miss Macayo, maybe I should've chosen different words. I do have a flair for dramatics as well, don't I?" He winks with a grin. "She and Martin went on their cruise, and she's enjoying herself too much to return. So she chose to retire."

I'm at a loss for words. There's no way she would have just retired. She is one of those people who desire the spotlight and would love a big ado about her retirement, especially since…

Wait. "Martin? I thought her husband's name is Roger." I ponder aloud. Martin Wray is the recently retired school music director. He was responsible for all of our production's accompaniments. Dr. Teague gives me a moment to put the pieces together. "Oh."

"I guess it was better for her to make a smaller exit than face the music, so to speak."

Wow. How did I not put two and two together when I was a student or when I helped out as her assistant director? All those nights I was encouraged to go home and left the two of them together.

"Well, that still leaves us an opening in the department," Dr. Teague presses on. "And I know it's less than a week for you to catch up on the syllabus, but since you're already known in the drama part of it."

I bite my lower lip. I have gotten so comfortable teaching Algebra to the newer students, getting to know them, and building a rapport with them, that this change would definitely alter my teaching style.

After not receiving an immediate response, Dr. Teague's eyes light up. "However, if you are concerned that you will not have time to assimilate yourself with the curriculum, we can always just have you take over the two drama classes, and we'll spread her remaining classes with the other instructors."

I exhale loudly. "If the second option is a possibility, I would prefer it." My heart leaps in joy at the consideration of being the head of the drama department.

"Perfect. I can't think of anyone else but you taking over that area. You are the most logical choice to be in charge of the stage." A ding sounds from his computer and smartwatch, and he smiles. "And what excellent timing, the other party is ready to join us."

Other party? I am curious if one of the English teachers is going to enter to converse about the current scheduling. However, when Dr. Teague opens the doors, I hear a familiar cadence in the guest's voice. I drink my cooled-down coffee as I rack my brain for who this could be. The deeper voice of the new guest confirms his gender at least. Still, no one comes to mind.

Finally, Dr. Teague moves out of the way and enters the handsome man who is moving in on the second floor. I choke on my drink and silently reprimand myself for not putting on makeup or contacts. My new neighbor, on the other hand, looks refreshed with his hair slightly damp and has changed to newer jeans and a fitted t-shirt, showing off his slight muscles. Not very athletic, but one can tell that there is some definition. I lower my head, rushing to think of where I know him from.

"Coffee?" The headmaster asks his new guest.

"Yes, thank you, Andreas." He takes the chair next to mine and turns to me. I take a quick inhale of the scent of wood and citrus, smelling the soap he used recently, then reminding myself that I am a professional, before turning to him with a confident smile. His hazel eyes twinkle as he recognizes me. "Oh hello, again!"

Dr. Teague hands him his cup of joe. "Oh good, you remember each other."

"I'm sorry?" Did I misunderstand my boss? Remember each other?

"I think you must have been mistaken, Andreas," the younger man states. "We nearly collided this morning in our building, but I do not think I met her before. We haven't been formally introduced." He gives me a flattering smile.

"Actually you have. You went to this very same school at the same time."

I finally give the newcomer a more thorough look. His eyes are extremely intoxicating, and his lips are quite inviting. I want to run my fingers through his wavy brown hair. Wait, I'm supposed to try to figure out who he is, not memorize his features for my fantasies. Suddenly, I have a flashback from my student days, freshman year to be exact when I first laid eyes on a certain junior at our *Bye Bye Birdie* rehearsals.

"Luisa Macayo, Ryan Marks," Dr. Teague finally reintroduces us.

I shake his hand but quickly turn in the opposite direction as to avoid showing my red face. I wouldn't have to update his features; it would be more like modernizing them. Ryan is my high school crush, and from the looks of it, he is now my adult crush, too.

However, the way he looks at me tampers my enthusiasm. He doesn't know who I am. Figures.

"I'm sorry, I'm processing your name and beauty." He ponders. "Macayo… Macayo… I do believe I had a classmate with that last name."

"Angela," I whisper, closing my eyes, and taking a deep breath. Shocker. He remembers her, but not me.

"Yes, Angela… Are you her sister?"

I exhale slowly before turning back to him, nodding, not trusting my words at the moment.

The headmaster smiles gently. "Of course, you remember Angela. She was the valedictorian of your graduating class. Luisa was in the theater with you."

"Oh." He gives me another glance before taking a drink of his coffee. No reaction. Wonderful.

"You'll have the opportunity to work on the same stage again," our boss gleefully states. "Miss Macayo just agreed to take over the theater department."

The younger man smiles. "Congratulations."

"And as our new band and choir coordinator, you two will be working closely together."

"You're giving me too much credit, Andreas. I'm only helping out with performance band, but I am responsible for all the vocals classes." He takes another drink and grins at me.

"Welcome back," I reply.

He raises his cup and indicates I meet his cup. I join in. "Cheers."

"Wonderful! I knew you two would make a great duo." Dr. Teague beams.

CHAPTER 3

An hour after the meeting, I finally escape to my classroom. I text Mia right away.

> You won't believe who is moving in below me.
>
> RYAN MARKS!!!!! 😍

I am not expecting a response right away, since she's at work, so I turn on my laptop to play some music in the classroom and determine what to do with my backboard. Math memes? Formulas? I hear a knock on my door as I look in my supply cabinet. I hit my head on a higher shelf.

"Are you all right?" The deep voice behind me asks. I close my eyes. Ryan Marks.

I take a deep breath before responding, "Yes." I slowly back up with a few laminated posters from years past. Some slip out to the floor.

"It looks like you need help," he crouches to pick up some of the fallen decorations.

"Thanks." I place my pile on the back table and gesture to him to do the same.

"I want to apologize if I made you uncomfortable earlier."

I'm not entirely sure if he was talking about blocking the stairwell when I was in a hurry or if it was during the meeting. I shrug. "No need to apologize. There's nothing to be sorry about."

"I want to assure you that I look forward to working with you… and be your neighbor."

"Likewise."

My phone alerts me to a message.

"I'll leave your math posters," he says, slightly chuckling at a Keanu Reeves meme about algebra and pirates.

He exits. I look at my phone, and instead of texting me back, Mia leaves a voicemail. I put the audio on speaker and listen to the message as I go through the posters.

"Oh my God!" She screams the message so loudly it overpowers the music. "Your Ryan? Your Ryan from high school? Is he still as hot as you thought-"

I hear a snicker in the background and freeze in horror before turning off the phone immediately. I didn't want to turn around. The heat from my face indicates that it's bright red. This isn't happening.

The guest clears their throat. "I had forgotten to ask you if you could give me some tips about how to make my choir room more comfortable." Ryan is still in the classroom… or quickly returned.

I swallow hard. "Absolutely," I manage to squeak out the response.

"Lovely," he gives a slight chuckle. "I'll await with bated breath your suggestions. Until then, Miss Macayo."

I'm going to kill my best friend.

• • •

Looking around sometime mid-afternoon, I feel that my classroom is equally fun and functional to learn algebra and about each other. I often try to make sure this is comfortable environment, especially since many of these kids are experiencing life away from home for the first time. Sure, we have several local students as well (considering we're the only high school in town, the zoned public school is in the next town over), but some of these kids, well-off or not, face a shock when they arrive here. I want them to know my classroom is a safe place.

With that thought in mind, I take my bag and head to the parking lot. However, before walking to the faculty lot, I pause and change the course to the arts building instead. I enter the newer structure with a big grin. It always feels right to be in this place. That I belong. That I'm home. I open the auditorium doors from the back of the house and take a deep breath. I am genuinely excited to be in charge of the productions. I need to confirm a few things with Dr. Teague and discuss with Ryan about shows.

I get to work with Ryan again. I know he doesn't remember me in the shows, and to be fair, being two years younger, I was cast as an ensemble member for *Bye Bye Birdie*; Penelope to be exact, while he got to play Mr. McAfee as a junior. However, I shocked everyone the following year by earning Ado Annie in *Oklahoma!* as a sophomore, and Ryan played Curly, the lead. Thinking back, I honestly believe he could give Hugh Jackman a run for his money in that role.

Deciding to simply focus on the stage tomorrow, I walk to the music corridor. Although I am familiar with the walk, I still read the name plaques for each room. The choir room doesn't show his name on it, but I know precisely which room it is. I enter the large room with built-in risers and a grand piano at the front. I smile as I recall the many times the cast would do rip-offs in here during our rare downtimes; the kids still do that today, and sometimes I'm tempted to join in.

I head to the choir master's private office but stop in my tracks as I hear voices in the small room. Cautiously glancing in, I see Ryan speaking to a young faux tan woman with bleached blonde dyed hair. She is cooing and flirting with him, touching his arm, and laughing very loudly. Ryan's expression seems to enjoy the company he has with his effortless smile affecting both the young lady and myself.

I know I shouldn't be jealous or even be frightened of whomever this person is. However, if he couldn't even remember me from before, I guess I am not good enough to be memorable in the first place. I don't stand a chance now. I turn around and head to the parking lot without letting him know I was there.

CHAPTER 4

Unsure if I want to bump into him in our shared living property, I drive to Mia's and Wesley's house. It's a small abode on the edge of town. Mia and Wesley have been together since she was still a student at Wellingworth; he is one of the few local kids who graduated from the zoned high school. And because love is love, they're still going strong for over a decade.

Of course, guests don't always have to wait for their host to let them in, unlike the apartment. In fact, I have a key that I never use, but they ask me to have it for emergencies, which is very responsible of them.

Today, however, the door was unlocked and Baskin, their geriatric rescue, stomps over to me. I know he's having a difficult time so I meet him halfway to give him some love.

"Honey, I'm home," I jokingly call out.

"In here, darling!" Mia's voice drifts from the kitchen. I stroll over there and find Mia slaving over a hot stove. Well, more like, preheating the oven for a frozen lasagna. Wesley is eating a bowl of cereal as he awaits his actual dinner.

"Awwww… you guys didn't have to cook for me." I jest.

Wesley grins. "Well, I told Mia that she has to start teaching you to be a properly kept woman now that the love of your life is back."

I groan, plopping down on the stool. "Yeah… well, it seems like a lost my chance already."

"Oh boy," Wesley expresses. "It sounds like girl talk. Not interested." He grabs his bowl and scoots behind Mia, giving her a quick squeeze on the butt before heading to their room.

Mia looks at me and sighs. "You've given up already?"

I shake my head. "I don't even think I had a shot. He doesn't remember me. I mean, I didn't recognize him right away either. I was in a hurry to make it to the meeting I had with Teague."

"So think of it as a fresh start, which is a good thing." The timer rings, and she places the lasagna on the rack and closes the door with her hip. "The prom fiasco didn't happen. The awkward staring that you did never occurred." She giggles to prevent me from arguing about that one. "Everything is new again. You can seduce him with your newfound confidence."

I snort. "Confidence? Now that's a joke."

"Isa, you are the long-time resident of this town, now, and he's the new kid. The roles are now reversed."

I think about that for a minute. "I have some more news."

"More tea? Spill!" She grabs a bottle of water from the fridge and slides it onto the counter for me.

"He teaches at Wellingworth now."

"Figures. The Fritzes only rent to the school staff."

"Old Joe doesn't work at the school," I remind her.

She shrugs. "Yeah, but they never would've allowed Wes and me to be there."

"But you guys have this awesome house to yourself! Backyard and rescue pups! Room to grow!"

Mia gives a smile that quickly turns into a scowl. "You got off subject. We're talking about you and Ryan Marks."

I almost point out that she began talking about housing but think better of it. "By the way, you're looking at the new drama department head!" I announce proudly.

My best friend squeals and rushes over to hug me! "Love and career upgrades!"

I hold a hand up. "Who said anything about love?"

She shakes her head. "Oh, Isa, why do you always have to be so cynical and closed off?"

"I'm not closed off."

"You also said you aren't confident."

"I'm not."

"But you now have this rare opportunity for second chances with a potential lover, someone you've admired for so long."

"Okay… wait a second. I pretty much forgot about him when I went off to college."

"Fair, but his return also relit some flames inside of you, didn't it?"

I groan, but she's not too far off. "I think the fire is too burnt out to be reignited."

"You have to let go of what happened in L.A. You deserve so much more, and no one will take it away from you this time. I'll make sure of it."

"Easy for you to say," I sigh. "But there's so much more…"

"I'm all ears," Mia drinks from the water bottle she gave me earlier.

"He remembers Angela."

She scowls again. "Of course, he'll remember Angela. They had classes together for four years. You only had two years of drama and chorus with him." I frown. "And despite how your family treats you, you are better than your sister. You got back on your feet after the west coast debacle and proved to be an excellent teacher and drama queen." She grins. "And this is without their assistance. So I think they're jealous that you are succeeding on your own without them. And that is something to be proud of."

I take in her words. Although Mia has said similar words before to try to get me out of my funk, I have always been reserved about taking them to heart. But I guess now I do have something to prove to myself and maybe gain Ryan Marks's admiration as I do so. I hug my best friend, just as Wesley comes of out the room. "Oh good. The preseason game's on. You staying for dinner, Iz?"

• • •

I forgot to tell Mia about the blonde in Ryan's office, but I figure that could wait. I leave shortly after Wesley returned to the kitchen, telling them to enjoy a romantic night together. Their faces suggest something I don't want to be a part of. As I drive back to my apartment, I ponder Mia's words. Have I really been closed off all these years?

I park my car at the back of the edifice and begin my two flights of stairs trek up to the third floor. I don't linger on the second floor, just in case. I have to figure things out before I can face him again, even if there is no chance of a relationship. However, his handsome face dominates my mind again when I see a note on my door.

> Miss Macayo, I tried to see if you were able to help me with the decor of the choir room this evening, but you aren't around. I hope we can talk more soon.
>
> RM

CHAPTER 5

The following morning the alarm buzzes at 6:00 am, which is my typical time during the school year. This time I take my time to look more presentable than I did yesterday. Full shower, blow dry, makeup, hand picking my clothes carefully. I tell myself this is not because of my new neighbor/coworker, but I'm done lying to myself.

After a quick breakfast, I descend the stairs but carefully looked around the corner on the second-floor landing before scurrying down that hall to the top of the next flight of stairs. Old Joe catches me, though, and chuckles. "Are you in a rush, Luisa?"

I give him a small wave before stepping down the final stairwell. I unlock the door to the utility/storage closet near the entrance and grab my bicycle. Adjusting my bag over my shoulders, I enjoy my ride to the school grounds.

My first stop allows me to drop off my bike in my math classroom, and it also gives me the opportunity to spritz up a bit to hopefully minimize the sweat. Once I feel more refreshed, I stuff my spare Bluetooth speaker in my bag and head to the auditorium in the arts building.

I let myself in backstage, turn on all the stage lights and open the main stage curtains. I step to the center and inhale deeply. My sanctuary. I turn on the Bluetooth speaker, connect my phone's musical playlist, and play a completely random show tune. Phillipa Soo's beautiful voice starts "Helpless" from *Hamilton*. Perfect.

Walking around the stage as if to breathe in the atmosphere, I start singing Eliza's part, lip-syncing Hamilton's and Angelica's portions, and creating my own choreography. When Hamilton's rap arrives, I continue to lip sync, but I hear a voice overriding Lin-Manuel Miranda's. Suddenly someone grabs my hand, and I turn to see Ryan Marks on one knee, singing… well, rapping along to be more precise. After a hot second to contain my shock, my training kicks in, and I embody Eliza completely and react accordingly.

We finish the song with flair. He presents his hands, encouraging me to take a bow to our imaginary audience, and I oblige before reciprocating the gesture, which he gladly does. He then takes my hand, and we bow together.

With Mamma Mia now playing, I grab my phone to turn off the music. He raises an eyebrow and claps gently. "That was exhilarating! I do miss being on stage."

"Me too," I concur.

"You are an excellent Eliza Hamilton, my dear," he takes my hand and kisses it. My face is warm again. I force myself to remember we are at school and that I'm a professional educator and actress.

"You're not so bad yourself, Alexander." I complement with an air of confidence (or so I hope).

"Well, I wasn't going to throw away my shot," he chuckles. I roll my eyes with a smirk. "It was probably going to be my only chance to ever play Hamilton. I don't think Mr. Miranda would ever want a white male to play the character, considering the tone of the show."

I shrug. "You're probably right, but stranger things have happened."

"Like a conservative high school producing RENT?"

"Augh…" I groan. "I am never going to unsee that, and they had some girl play Angel because they didn't want to have any of the guys cross-dress. It was a nightmare." I shiver. "Jonathan Larson would be rolling over in his grave. God rest his soul."

We laugh gently before an awkward silence descends on the stage. I feel as if he is looking me over again, and I'm doing my best to avoid eye contact, bringing myself back instead of a character from a show.

"Miss Macayo," he breaks the silence.

"Isa," I interject. "Luisa formally, but friends call me Isa."

He gives his very easy-going smile. "All right then, Isa."

"Mr. Marks?" I reply with a smile.

He laughs. "Mr. Marks is my father… actually, he's Ambassador Marks," he corrects himself wistfully. I take a glance at him and see a bit of frustration in his usually bright eyes. However, it disappears immediately. "I'm just Ryan"

I nod. "Okay, Ryan." I hope I didn't breathe out that name as I would've in the past. "But remember it needs to be Mr. Marks to the students, no matter their age."

"Thank you for the advice." He pauses. "Do you have time right now to give me more pointers for classroom decor and decorum? Or do you have more songs that you have to perform to make sure the acoustics in this place is as incredible as I heard them to be?" He looks around the stage before settling back to my face. "Honestly if there are more songs, I would like to participate in our own private revue. I cannot think of a more enjoyable way to pass the time." He winks at me. I'm surprised I'm still standing because I swear my knees have turned into gelatin.

I open my mouth, but because it became dry suddenly, no words come out. After clearing my throat, I manage to respond. "I have time."

"Superb," he grins at me. "I truly appreciate this, Isa. This is my first foray into educating, and I certainly do not want to create any disappointing results." I nod as we walk to the music hall.

"I understand what you're saying," I reassure him. "You'll do well. You have a good grasp of the subject. You have a great personality." You're incredibly gorgeous, and your voice is amazing. "Just use good judgment, build a professional rapport…"

"Of course. Good judgment. I imagine no fraternizing with colleagues falls into that category." I choke on my saliva. He turns around with concern. I give him a thumbs up and bite my bottom lip as soon as he proceeds to his classroom.

"Wha... what makes you say that?" I stammer. In the back of my mind, I'm praying that he finally notices me.

He holds the door open to his classroom, welcoming me into it. "As students, my mates and I always figured some of our teachers were.... shall we say.... shagging, to be blunt." I swallow. He shrugs. "Small town, not much else to do."

Or someone else to do, I think back to yesterday's revelation of Georgette Stein and Martin Wray's infidelities. I feel for their significant others. I sigh.

He looks at me curiously, "Penny for your thoughts?"

"Huh?" I look startled.

He chuckles. "It appears you were lost in thought."

I laugh but feel the heat in my face rise. "I... I was just...." I look around the large room that I had visited the day before and decide to avoid what is really on my mind. "There is a lot you can do here."

Ryan chuckles. "Right. A lot of room for music-based paraphernalia."

"Exactly. Just make sure you put a little of yourself into it, make it personal."

"Like Neo stating that algebra teachers are pirates?"

I squint my eyes at him. "First of all, that was Ted from Bill and Ted's Excellent Adventure. Secondly... how do you know I'm not a pirate?"

He holds his arms up in surrender. "My apologies, Captain Isa!" He looks at me thoroughly again and after a beat, asks. "Why do you teach math? You definitely belong on stage."

I look into his eyes, and those hazel orbs are truly seeking the truth. "That's a bit of a long story. But the short ver-"

The door to the classroom slams loudly, and in saunters the blonde from yesterday. I look at the young girl carefully. Zoey Waines is a former student who is now at Wellingworth after a marginal modeling career. She believes herself to be an influencer but "earns" money as a resident advisor in the newest dormitory on campus, which is named for the donors, her family.

"Oh, Ryan," she coos as she enters, but her face turns into a scowl upon seeing me. "Mi... Luisa," she grits her teeth. "What are you doing here?'

"I've asked her to give me some assistance with turning this room into a good learning environment." Ryan smiles at me.

Zoey laughs. "She is so out of touch with today's kids. I graduated only a few years ago from here AND I live with them. You should've asked me." She touches his arm seductively. "I can help with ANYTHING you need."

I may have been biting my lip a little longer and harder than I should have since I taste a little bit of blood. Of course, his question about fraternizing is about Zoey, the 23-year-old who once modeled for Victoria's Secret. I take a deep breath and give them a professional smile while avoiding Ryan's eyes. "She is familiar with that age group. I can't argue with that. I've got some more preparation to do. You both have a good day."

Zoey grins victoriously. "Bye," she shoos me away with sarcasm. I hear her fawning over Ryan as I leave the room, "Oh, Ry-Ry, I can already picture how chic this room could be!"

I quietly close the door and lean against it. Frustrated, I remind myself I am better than they say I am. I'm doing this for me. I pray silently. "God grant me the serenity to accept the things I cannot change, the courage to change the things I can, and the wisdom to know the difference."

CHAPTER 6

Instead of returning to the auditorium, I walk back to my math classroom. I want to distance myself from what just occurred, and I need to process everything.

When I get there, a vase with a beautiful array of flowers is on the desk, along with a card from the English department, congratulating me for taking over the drama department. Along with their signature, each teacher wrote a personalized note of encouragement and enthusiasm, and I take it as a sign of approval of my advancement. Nearby an envelope with Jane Tromberg's distinct handwriting contains the theater office key and a note asking me to check my email for my new class schedule.

The schedule is more packed than I initially anticipated. My planning periods are replaced with the two drama classes; my classes are back to back all week with lunch as my only break for the day. Dr. Teague emails that he will talk to the head of the math department to determine if we can move things around to provide me with a planning period, but as of right now, I'm stuck with the schedule as it is.

I use a spreadsheet program to create a schedule and color coordinate how much time to get between the two buildings when a slight rap disrupts the room's silence. Ryan Marks is at the door.

"Am I interrupting?" He holds up my Bluetooth speaker. "You left this on the stage." He enters and puts it on my desk before sitting on a tabletop of a student's desk.

"Thanks." I attempt a small smile.

"Don't mention it," he replies.

I pretend to ignore him but occasionally peer over my screen to see him go to the backboard that I completed yesterday.

"You finished it," he happily observes. "I see the Neo-" he pauses and looks back at me. I raise my eyebrows, preparing to correct him. "I mean, Ted 'Theodore' Logan meme passed and is featured."

I stand up and head toward the door. "I wouldn't say featured, just like I wouldn't say I have a favorite integer or variable I use."

He chuckles. "That's not true. We all have favorites, number, show, et cetera." He meets me at the door. "Are you trying to get rid of me?"

"I have to go to the faculty lounge to get what I printed out."

"Mind an escort?"

We walk quietly down the hall. After a moment of silence, we both break it.

"I find it..." I begin.

"So I was..." he starts. We look at each other and smile. "Ladies first."

"Mine wasn't very important," I look down at my steps.

"You wouldn't say unless it wasn't so. It must be important to you."

I shake my head. "Not really. I was just going to comment on how impressed I was that you learned Keanu's full character name."

He stops, forcing me to stop and glance at him. "I find it important then! A compliment is always an important thing, especially coming from a beautiful colleague." I roll my eyes, but inside I pick apart the latter part of the statement. What did he mean? Probably just saying it to be polite. Don't look too much into it, Isa!

"Don't roll your eyes," he mockingly reprimands me. "You know it to be true."

"That compliments are important? Of course… we all need to build each other up instead of bringing each other down." I turn to the larger classroom-turned-faculty lounge that looks over an enclosed courtyard.

He follows me in. "For the record, I looked that up on IMDb. Care to join me in watching it tonight on the telly."

Before I begin to analyze his invitation, a groan arises from the middle of the room. One of the science teachers, Sebastian Fontier, is sitting there, I presume taking a break. He is the living epitome of Professor Snape from the Harry Potter series and Grumpy Cat rolled into one.

"Sebastian!" Ryan exclaims. "How are you doing, mate?"

He glares at him. "Honestly do they allow anyone to instruct here? This institution is going downhill." Sebastian gives a tsk before, leaving the room.

I watch the whole thing with confusion. "What just happened?"

Ryan only shakes his head. "I don't think he has forgiven me yet…"

"Forgiven you?" I scan my ID at the copier, bringing the machine to life. "What did you do? Steal his girlfriend?" I chortle as I swipe the screen for my work.

The machine processes my papers. "Not his girlfriend… Did he ever have a girlfriend?" Ryan asks me. "Or a boyfriend? Or have an orientation of some sort?" I shrug.

"Then it's probably much worse in his mind." He leans on the copier. "I bettered him while we attended here."

"Meaning you had a better GPA?" I grab papers that the machine spits out.

"Meaning I was the salutatorian of our graduating class by just a few points."

I begin warming up the laminating equipment as I look over my schedule chart. I know very little about my fellow teacher except that he is very salty and bitter. The students often complain about how dry his presentations and subject are. "From what I know he didn't do too bad himself. Rumor has it that he worked for NASA for a bit. Still don't know how he got to teach here." I sway on the balls of my feet as I prepare my paperwork to become another chart in my classroom. "I hear he's a stickler for grades and procedures and whatnot."

Ryan chuckles. "Some things never change."

As the paper laminates, I turn the tables back to him. "You never did say what you wanted to say earlier."

He ponders for a moment, cautiously holding the edge of the heated laminated paperwork. He reads it and whistles loudly. "This is your class schedule?"

The second sheet is getting plastic heated on it. I sigh. "Yeah. I guess they decided to just take away my planning periods to teach theater. I'm hoping we can find a solution because this is overwhelming."

"I can imagine," he comments, giving me a sympathetic look.

I shrug before asking him again. "So why are you avoiding what you were about to say earlier? Does it have anything to do with Zoey?"

"Pardon?" he blinks a couple of times and shakes his head. "No, nothing like that."

I stay silent as I complete my task and wait for him to continue. He finally speaks. "I feel as if I'll be adding more stress."

"I did it to myself. I agreed to take charge of the theater on top of my regular duties." I look at him anticipating his thoughts.

"It's just you and I need to get together." I raise my eyebrows. He pauses and laughs. "I mean, we need to talk about the productions."

Of course, it is about working together. He doesn't even remember me from his student days, which makes me think that he wouldn't think of me otherwise. "You only need to worry about the winter showcase and the spring musical. I can handle the fall production."

He takes another glance at one of my laminated schedules. "You need help, Isa. Your days are quite full."

I take the chart from him. "I made that decision. I wasn't forced into it." I head out of the lounge.

He follows me. "I didn't mean to imply that you were. I'm just saying I'm here if you need help."

I turn around to face him before I enter my classroom. "I appreciate that. But I think you have your hands full with acclimating as a first-year teacher…" And Zoey Waines.

He sighs. "All right," he backs off a bit, but then takes out his phone. My phone buzzes; he digitally sends me his contact info. I accept the file, but he looks, waiting. I sigh and text him. He grins. "No excuses. Now I won't have to tape messages on your door." I smile. "Farewell, my dear Eliza." He bows and finally makes his way back to the arts building.

CHAPTER 7

Wednesday morning means only one day before the boarding students arrive, and most of the faculty and staff are on edge, naturally. I haven't had a chance to prep anything on the stage, but my best friend had a brilliant idea. "Just use your regular classroom for the two drama classes… move the desks and work around that setup for both algebra and theater. Killing two birds with one stone: You don't have to move around as much and avoid getting distracted by a certain person."

So I meet with the counselors to advise them of the change in the classroom assignment. They are apprehensive of the change and attempt to undermine my decision, stating the rooms in the main building wouldn't have the capacity to hold those classes, that I need to get the administration's permission, etc. For the first time in seven years, I hold my ground. Typically I am easy to deal with, usually upholding what is provided without any complaints; however, with no breaks other than lunch, I need to make this convenient for me. I need to make it work.

• • •

Move-in Thursday launches the school year. The boarding and local students take the opportunity to catch up with their old friends they haven't seen all summer. However, with social media and cell phones, I know they have been communicating with one another; they would hate living in the times when I was a student there.

I'm providing information at the drama table between the two first-year residence halls, encouraging kids to enrich their lives with the arts. We welcome everyone to get involved in the big productions and do not limit participation to those enrolled in the theater classes.

Kimberly Jensen and Bryce Billings approach the table. These two juniors have assisted in many performances, and from their closeness, I believe the student talk of the two getting together.

"Hi, Miss Macayo!" The teen girl goes behind the table to hug me. The other student stands on the other side but gives me a big smile.

After a short hug, I ask them about their summer.

"Worked," Bryce answers. He's one of the local kids that attends on a scholarship and is a brilliant student. I hear he's looking at some of the Ivy League schools. "I was… am still a busboy at Floriente. Have you been, Miss M?"

I shake my head. "No, I haven't had an opportunity."

"Well, if you ever want to, let me know. I may be low on the totem pole, but I still have some pull." He grins proudly.

I nod before turning to his girlfriend. "And Kim? How was the move-in day?"

She shifts her weight and glances at Bryce for a brief moment. I don't think she wanted me to catch that. "It went well," she states slowly and returns to the other side of the table.

Okay, I think to myself. Something's up. They'll tell me when they're ready.

"So what ancient shows did Stein…" I raise my eyebrows. I taught all the students to call their elders by their proper titles respectfully. "I mean, Mrs. Stein reserve for us this year?" Kim asks casually as if the previous moment hadn't occurred.

"Actually," I pause for effect. "There is a new person at the wheel…"

"Huh?" Bryce looks puzzled. Kim shrugs.

"A new sheriff in town?" I suggest. Both teens shake their heads, still confused.

I sigh. "Mrs. Stein retired."

They inhale and grin. "So the old bag finally did it," Bryce comments gleefully. Kim slaps him playfully. "Sorry, Miss M…. But let's face it, she was OOOOOOO-LD! She was born during Jurassic Age or something."

While I attempt to show my displeasure about his not-so-flattering comments, I can't help but provide a small smile of agreement.

Kim ponders for a moment before speaking, "With both S- Mrs. Stein and Mr. Wray gone, does that mean?" She looks at me with hope.

I nod with a smile. "You're looking at your new drama director."

The teen girl runs back around and engulfs me in a bigger hug. She's jumping up and down at the news. "Oh my goodness! I'm so thrilled!"

Her boyfriend agrees wholeheartedly. "Yes! You totally deserve it, Miss M!"

"So you're not just teaching freshmen anymore, right? I mean, you got your hands full with the acting classes and choir?" Kim assume.

"I'm pulling double duty but not for choir."

"But you just said…"

"I said I'm the new drama head," I explain. "I'm only taking over the two acting courses Mrs. Stein had for this year. They hired someone to take over Mr. Wray's music department. Two someones, actually." I recall a woman I met at end of the year during Martin's retirement shindig at the end of last year. "I guess they're splitting the band, orchestra, and vocals classes?"

"You could've totally taken over the vocal section," Bryce responds.

"Yeah, you have a great voice," Kim offers.

"Thanks, but Mrs. Stein's retirement came as a shock to all of us. And at the very last minute." I shrug. "So they ask me to handle the theater end of things. I'm still teaching algebra."

"Wow, you're my hero," Kim smiles.

"Sure if you don't want to have a life." I pause as the words slip out of my mouth. I didn't mean to say to my students. Or maybe subconsciously, I wanted to let them know how much I do for them.

The two teens give me appreciative but sad looks. "We are really grateful for all you do," Bryce comments.

"Thanks, B," I grin.

• • •

I receive an email late Thursday night. Dr. Teague is asking me to come at 8:00 am with no other details on the meeting. My anxiety is heightened. At 2:00 am, I finally get to an uneasy sleep.

CHAPTER 8

I wake up an extra half hour early to prepare for the talk. I'm still nervous when I head down the stairs at 7:15 am. Ryan opens his door, just as I make it to the landing. Wearing just boxers and a plain t-shirt, his hair is a mess, and he has a slight stubble and sleepy eyes. I lick my lips; he looks incredibly sexy.

I exhale. "Hey."

"Good morning, sunshine." He yawns and stretches, making the t-shirt rise a little, showing a little of his abs. I pray I'm not physically drooling. "What was all the commotion upstairs about?"

"Was I making too much noise?" I inquire. "Sorry."

"Don't be, love." There was a pause.

"I have a meeting with Dr. Teague."

"Another one?" That perks his interest even more.

"I know… two in one week. I wonder what I did wrong this time."

He shakes his head. "Nothing…. From what everyone tells me, you're a perfect example of what a cool teacher and coworker should be."

My eyebrows go up. He's been asking around about me. I want to ask more, but I don't want to be late. "I'll…. Um…. I'll see you around."

He nods with a smile before closing the door, and I bound down the last flight of stairs.

• • •

I enter the main office suite with plenty of time. Jane Tromberg still needs to arrive at her desk, or maybe she just step out. Her desk was a disaster, more than usual. I sit at one of the chairs to wait.

She arrives with one of the counselors shadowing her. When they see me, Jane gives me a small smile, not entirely friendly. The counselor just frowns. This makes me more anxious than before. There is tension in the air providing an uncomfortable silence while we wait for the headmaster.

After twenty minutes, five minutes past the set meeting time, the door finally open. Several department heads came out. I catch the eyes of the math department head; he scowls. This is not off to a good start. The only positive reaction I receive is from the arts department head, who gives me a thumbs up and a genuine friendly smile. The headmaster appears after all the instructors leave. He nods at me to enter the office; I stand immediately and walk in. I await his lead to determine what to do next. He closes the door and motions me to sit at the same spot from earlier this week.

"Thank you for coming in again," Dr. Teague begins. There is an edge of exhaustion in his voice.

"You're welcome?" I apprehensively respond. He nods so I add, "Are you all right, sir?"

"Honestly, a lot has occurred over the past twenty-four hours."

"Oh," I'm not sure what I have to do with it.

"Good developments," he expands. "It's just the timing could have been better."

"Um… okay." I'm unsure how to respond.

"I'll be frank, Miss Macayo," he finally sits down across from me. I freeze. He's going to ask me to step down away from the theater. Or worse, he's going to fire me. For what? For avoiding the stage? For moving the acting classes to a math classroom? I wish I know what was going on.

"The counseling staff has been inundated with last-minute requests to add theater classes. Apparently, the students have learned that Georgette has retired and you are now responsible for the productions and the classes."

I feel flush. Was the Stein retirement confidential? I know I didn't reveal how the decision came about to anyone, not even Mia. I ramble out an apology. "I didn't know that Georgette's retirement wasn't made public."

He forces a chuckle. "Actually the board and most of the staff knew of it before I offered you the position. So that news has probably been spread online before you ever entered the building." I nod. "And the people privy to that information were all in agreement to ask you to take control of the theater. You were the obvious choice." I once again nod, not knowing if I had the words to reply.

"But we didn't anticipate how big the reaction would be from the student body. The student surveys have always suggested that you're a teacher they can connect with, and parents have also expressed how their children comprehend algebra with only one semester with you.

"So the plan was to slowly integrate you as the head of that program if you chose not to move to the English department. We were going to get someone to take over two of your algebra one classes so you can have a break." Dr. Teague takes a deep breath. "But as of yesterday afternoon, the requests have reached the point that we can fill three more classes including those who are already on the waitlist for the program. It seems, Miss Macayo, that the students want someone who they truly want to learn from; someone, whom some have stated, that doesn't only live in the last century."

I stifle a giggle at that last statement. Being a theater director for decades, including when I was a student, Georgette uses the same shows on a rotation. She was confident with those shows and never truly considered any newer shows. Both the students and I express the same frustration when she announces the same shows over and over again.

"So with all this in mind, the board in their infinite wisdom informed me that the integration plan is out, and you will be responsible for a whole section on your own."

I look at the headmaster, still somewhat confused. "I'm sorry, sir, but I'm not entirely sure I comprehend what you are saying."

"You, Miss Macayo, will be teaching three additional theater classes, for a total of five theater classes and bear the burden of the whole new theater section."

I bite my lip. "What about the algebra classes?"

He shakes his head with a chuckle. "You are always the one to make sure everything is covered. We will redistribute your classes with the other math teachers, which was option number one when we first gave you this opportunity."

I sigh, trying to absorb all of this knowledge, once again being changed at the last minute. "So these new classes?"

"Your new class schedule will take effect on Monday, as planned. I know this is yet another change from what we initially discussed earlier, but the board, the parents, and the students made it quite clear that this is what they want."

I close my eyes. It is Friday morning, and the first day of school is Monday. I have prepared nothing for my theater classes, figuring I would have this weekend to simply create a syllabus for two classes, not five.

"I know I should be flattered that they would want me to be their teacher and all," I finally state. "But I feel like this is all too much."

Dr. Teague nods. "I understand."

I sigh loudly. "I guess the decision has been made then, about how this is going to be for the year."

"Well, there is one other thing," the headmaster interjects. "You don't need your current classroom anymore. I can ask the custodians to help bring your personal items to your new studio and office in the arts building. And you will have access to the rooms all weekend, so you'll be prepared Monday morning for your first class." I nod.

"Don't worry, Miss Macayo, we know you'll be a success in this new role. We all believe in you."

CHAPTER 9

Although I am excited about my new teaching post, I feel like a burden to the math, arts, and counseling departments. To help alleviate some of this weight, I printed out about two months' worth of lesson plans from my past years of teaching algebra and left some worksheets to help out whoever will take over that course. I also choose not to ask the custodians for help, except to borrow a maintenance cart and two or three boxes to dump all my personal items into. It only takes me one trip from the main building to the arts edifice to move what I leave in my classroom regularly.

After the drop-off, I look around the very large studio classroom assigned to me. It contains the same functions as the other classrooms: a large whiteboard, a projector, a screen, built-in speakers, bulletin boards, student desks, tables, bookshelves, etc. I frown at no cabinet space or no teacher's desk. I guess I use the theater office backstage for personal items. However, the roller coaster of emotions and the physical move finally affect me. I return the cart and head back to my apartment, knowing I have the weekend to set up the classroom properly.

• • •

I hit my bed as soon as I get home. It's been a long week, and I won't get much sleep, let alone take a nap on a weekday, once Monday arrives.

• • •

I am awakened by my buzzing cell phone. I answer groggily. "Hello?"

Mia's voice responds. "Hey! I'm downstairs. I brought nourishments!"

I try to see the time. With the sun setting, I can guess it's pretty late afternoon or early evening, but I am unsure. "I'll be down in a minute." I stretch and turn on the light in the living room on the way out of the apartment. I bound down the stairs, still not lingering long on the second floor, and reach the door. Mia is standing with a two-liter of Dr. Pepper and a large pizza. I open the door and welcome her in.

"That was longer than a minute," she jokes. "Your hair looks like a rat's nest."

I groan. "It has been a long day." We walk up the stairs and make it to the second landing just as Ryan opens the door. He's all dressed up, looking extremely hot in a suit. Suddenly I feel self-conscious, especially with Mia's comment about my hair.

"Good evening, Isa!" He greets me and nods at Mia with a smile. "Hello!"

"Um…" I shake myself, forcing myself to focus on the here and now. "Ryan Marks, Mia Cartwright, Mia, Ryan." She shoves the pizza box and the soda to me and wipes her hands on her jeans before offering one to my neighbor.

"Nice to meet you," She coos.

"Pleasure," he responds during the handshake. "You attended Wellingworth as well, did you not?"

I hold back a groan. Wonderful, he remembers her but not me. Mia nods cheerfully. "I certainly did. Good memory."

"So do you ladies have any amazing plans tonight?" He asks politely, looking at the pizza.

"Just catching up. Haven't had a chance to chit chat my bestie," Mia answers.

He massages his neck. "Yeah, it's been a crazy week. I have a newfound respect for teachers now." He returns his focus to me. "I stopped by your classroom this afternoon, it was completely empty. Even the Ted meme was gone."

"Oh… um… Yeah, I was reassigned to the arts building." I explain, shifting my weight back and forth between my feet.

"I wish you had texted me. I would have liked to help you move."

"And is your classroom ready?" I quip back. Mia gives me a side glance, surprised at my confrontational tone.

"That room was pretty much set before I even got there," he shrugs. "I'll get a feel of my choruses' personalities and go from there."

"Didn't Zoey say she can help you with that?" I say curtly. Mia shoots daggers at me, telling me to stop.

"Er…." he adjusts his tie nervously. "She may have mentioned something along those lines. Honestly, that girl says quite a bit of things."

Mia nudges me upstairs. "Pizza's getting cold," she hissed.

"Course" I give Ryan a tight smile. "Have fun on your date!"

As Mia and I walk over the second flight of stairs, I swear I heard him say, "I wouldn't call it a date."

We get to my door, and I fumble with the key nervously before Mia exasperatedly grabs the food from me. Once we're through the door, Mia slams the food on the counter. "Would you care to explain what the hell that was all about?! If that was your idea of flirting, you failed miserably."

I lean back on my door as she grabs plates and glasses from the cabinet. "And who the hell is this Zoey chick?"

I sigh. I take the plate with a slice that she offers me, and I fill her in on the events of this week. Once I finish, she stops chewing her second slice of pizza and glares at me thoughtfully. "So this is what you've been holding back? A new classroom and some entitled brat who seems to have daddy issues?"

I swallow my first bite. "To be fair, the new classroom was just assigned to me today. I just started stressing about that a few hours ago."

She shakes her head. "Okay, Isa, you know I love you, but you really gotta stop allowing people to get the best of you! Your mom, your sister, and now this floozy…"

"Floozy? Did we travel back in time a hundred years? Plus, I had that longing thing under control until tonight." I bury my head in my hands.

"Did you really?"

"With Ryan? Yes! I was having professional and neighborly conversations with him over the last few days."

"So… what happened?"

"He looked really good tonight," I start.

"I'll agree to that," Mia says with a playful grin. "He grew up well. Not as handsome as my Wesley, but for your standards…"

I smirk. "Yeah… well, dressing up to go out on a Friday night means you're trying to impress someone… usually a date…"

"Remember what they say about assuming things," she begins.

"It makes an ass of you and me," we say in unison. We look at each other and jug the remaining sodas from our respective cups. She burps loudly, and I snort laughing.

"I can be there tomorrow to make sure your studio is ready,"

I shake my head. "I can't have you do that. You do so much for me already."

"Pish posh," Mia replies. "We are best friends; we've always got each other's backs."

"You sound like a character from an after-school special or rom-com." I refill our cups with soda.

"Sometimes I feel like we are in one…"

• • •

True to her word, Mia assists me in getting my new classroom ready in a matter of hours, which would've probably taken me all weekend if I was on my own. I treat her to a late afternoon coffee at the cafe. We are discussing the upcoming school year when Zoey leads a group of young teenage girls to the bistro. I nod to Mia, who looks back to the extremely obnoxious newcomers. She shows a neutral expression, but her eyes roll.

"I'm paying for all my residents!" Zoey says loudly to ensure the whole place hears. Most of the other patrons simply ignore what's happening; Mia and I look at one another and silently agree to look casual.

"They allow me to post about their cute creations and people come here because they follow me on social media!" The young adult continues, hoping to garner more attention. "And my boyfriend lives right upstairs so I'll be able to do this a lot more now!"

That final statement gets my attention, but before I could react, Mia grabs my hand and squeezes it. She shakes her head. Do not engage. Do not take anything she says at face value.

"Did I tell you girls I model, too?" Zoey brags as they find some tables in the corner. "And you know your dorm is named after me!"

Mia and I catch each other's eyes and snicker.

"Girls, just stick with me and learn important lessons that will carry you through life. The school will only teach you stuff that you won't need in the real world. Me? I will give you all my knowledge about how it really is out there." Some of the girls sigh in admiration loudly.

My best friend and I take a drink in unison, trying not to groan. This girl is certifiable.

• • •

My final Sunday of summer break finds me making massive Amazon purchases and creating a contact information sheet for my students. When I go in the morning, I make a mental note to print out the class roster and my new schedule (two classes on one day, three on alternating days).

I begin to research different textbooks I can use for class when my video messenger pops up. My family is at their regular weekly dinner. Wonderful. I plaster a smile on my face before opening the app.

"Oh Katherine, you are so smart! You make this working for your Tita[7] Luisa," my mother's hairline is all I can see.

"Lola[8], you need to sit down so Tita Isa can see you," my oldest niece insists.

She finally sits down like a queen on the couch.

"Luisa, you need to call us more," my mother greets me. "I'm old and will die soon." Dramatic as always. I guess that's why I have a knack for performing.

"Nanay[9], tomorrow is the first day of school. I've been busy all week," I explain. It's as if they don't understand how valuable and tedious teaching is.

"Make sure you eat… but not too much," my mom warns. "You only eat for you. You need to find a boy and make babies and then you can eat for two."

I wince at her comment, "I hear you."

My sister appears behind her with a devious grin. "So I got the back-to-school edition of the alumni newsletter yesterday. And you were featured."

"Oh?" I haven't said anything about my promotion

"Head of the drama department?" My sister spills the news.

---

[7] Filipino translation: a title for aunt

[8] Filipino translation: a title for grandmother

[9] Filipino translation: mother

"What happened to the nice lady was before?" My mom asks, overlooking the good news of her daughter earning a bigger position.

"Mrs. Stein," Angela responds.

"Yes… yes, she is a nice lady. Did a good job. Give Luisa a job."

I hold back a sigh. "Well, now, I'm the one in charge of that, Nanay! They promoted me Friday!"

"Oh no, no, no, no," my mom starts. "Too much work for you."

I am about to say something, but once again, Angela speaks. "That's not all, is it, Isa? I read that my old classmate is the new choir chair, Ryan Marks."

"Yes, he is," I confirm.

"Didn't you have a huge crush on him?" She smirks.

"No sex until you're married!" My mother contributes.

What?! I'm at a complete loss; how did this chat turn from my rise to theater director to Ryan and sex?!

"Who is Ryan Marks?" My mom muses.

"The British Ambassador's illegitimate child," Angela answers smugly. What does legitimacy have anything to do with it?

"He also happens to be the salutatorian of your class," I add, recalling the conversation Ryan and I had the other day.

"Yeah… Sebastian and I have always agreed that he pulled a fast one on Dr. Teague and the administration. I mean, he took easy courses like theater and music and became number two in the class… please."

I blanch, "A. He took the same difficult core classes as you. And B. I took those same classes!"

"And look at where you both are now," She pretends to do a mic drop and gives me a pretentious grin.

"Yes, yes, you can do better," my mom agrees. "Look at what Katherine is doing now. She is following in your Ate's footsteps. She's going to be a good doctor like her mommy." She gestures for my niece to come on the screen and forces me to endure another "Angela and family" show.

After about an half hour of boasting, I finally manage to end the video call by informing them that I have more things to prepare for tomorrow. I go to the kitchen and pour myself a glass of wine. Dealing with my family is more drama than anything I can direct on stage.

CHAPTER 10

For many teachers and students, the first day of the school year can cause a lot of panic. Even the most prepared will hit a snag sooner or later. Typically, I'm the prepared one, and I am very well versed in the subject matter and know how to present each lesson daily. While I'm quite comfortable with the art of acting and knew what to do on the first day of class, the lesson plans for the remainder of the year as well as the productions are still unknown to me. Those facts make me extremely nervous.

Thankfully with a theater class, I can project my favorite playlist all day. So after I turn on the Bluetooth speaker, I blast a familiar tune turned show number, "Hand in my Pocket." While singing along, I prepare for the new class by posting my newly updated schedule at the studio door, the backstage bulletin board hallway, and the theater office door. I open the office connecting door to the studio classroom to find Ryan also singing the song. He looks over at the newly open door, shocked about this secret door, but he grins as we sing to each other… well, up until the final chorus when a school bell rings and the show's character yells profanity at the interruption in the song.

"What happened to the taxi cab?" He is in complete shock.

"This is from *Jagged Little Pill*," I explain as I turn down the music.

"Right, it's a cover of the Alanis Morissette hit."

"It's from the 2018 Broadway show."

"Of course, you'd be playing your musical playlist," he smiles.

"It is a theater class," I retort.

"How long has this door been here?" He looks at the office, which was quite disorganized.

"Probably since this building has been built." I begin writing out the agenda for the day on the board. "Stein never used it."

"Are there any other cool features that my classroom doesn't have?" he begins to look around. I sigh as I complete my written instructions.

There is another door near the office, which I unlock for him to go through. Beyond the door are several decades of props from various shows. "The prop room?" His face looks like a child in a candy store as he enters, picking up random items. I can't help but giggle at his enthusiasm. He looks so cute.

He picks at a random cowboy hat and begins the final verse of "People Will Say We're in Love" from his final show at the school. I watch him in silence, recalling the show, and wonder if he remembers me from those days at all.

He pulls me by one hand and spins me around. "Don't dance all night with me. Till the stars fade from above." He pulls me close to him, his strong arms just above my waist.

"They'll see it's all right with me." He continues to sing, looking deeply into my eyes. "People will say we're in love." The final line is sung quietly. I take shallow breaths and take in his hazel eyes. His head slowly moves down to mine… a few millimeters before our lips touch, the school's real bell loudly blares in the studio, startling both of us. I back away, his stare never leaves me. "I… um… have things to get ready."

Ryan gulps and nods. "I do have a first-period class." He returns the hat and gives his easy-going smile. "You do have a pretty cool classroom, Isa. Have a good first day."

"You, too." I close the props room after he leaves the classroom. I am bewildered at what just happened.

• • •

I drive directly to Mia and Wesley's after school. I let myself in and make sure Baskin got some love. After looking around and finding no one in the living room, kitchen or backyard, I wonder why the front door is unlocked. Unless…

Oh gosh.

I walk to the foyer and was about to leave when Wesley walks out in just his underwear. My face probably looks like a tomato, and I turn away immediately. "Oh hey, Iz… hey babe, Isa's here!"

"Oh is she? I'll be out in a sec!"

"I didn't… I mean… I'll come back another time."

"Don't be silly. My sex goddess will be out here soon." I hear footsteps heading to the kitchen.

A moment later, Mia walks out, "Hey! Didn't know you were stopping by! How is the first day back?"

Still a little flustered, I shrug. "Same old, same old."

She snorts. "I'm not buying it, and why are you just standing there? Do you want to go to the kitchen?"

"No!" I exclaim immediately. I do not want to traumatize myself again.

"Okay, then, why don't you sit in the chair here?" I do as I am asked, keeping my head down. "What's with you?"

The footsteps return from the kitchen, and Mia giggles and gives her significant other a loud kiss. "It's called sex, Isa. And if I recall correctly you are not immune from activity."

It's true. When did I turn out to be such a prude? Maybe it's because I haven't had action in years, or am I just confused about my high school crush?

"Get out of here, you love god, you!" Another kiss can be heard. "We can continue..."

I groan. "Okay, stop, please!"

Both of them chuckle. After a beat, Wesley bids me farewell before returning to their room or the family room.

"You can look up now," Mia states. "I'm pretty moderately dressed. Plus you were my roommate so I'm sure you've seen me in a worse state. At least I'm blissfully happy."

I look up but choose not to look at her, my eyes darting around the room.

"So are you going to tell me the truth, or do I have to pillow it out of you?" I know she's prepared to throw a pillow at me.

"You guys still going to the game Friday?" I stall.

"Yes, but you're dragging out the inevitable, so you might as well come out with now." A pillow hits my arm, finally forcing me to look at her, who thankfully is a bit more conscientious than her partner. "Remember I know all your tricks."

I sigh. This morning's incident is on repeat in my mind, not a bad distraction, but it's a distraction nonetheless. I only manage to get through classes because I feel like I'm performing a role, which should never be the case.

Instead, I share my family's video conversation with her. This time she sighs. "Seriously this is not normal. Not that I had what I consider a normal childhood, but your family will cause anyone to go psycho. I won't be too shocked if you go all Lizzy Borden on them."

I stare at her and shrug nonchalantly. "If the sight of blood and the thought of violence didn't make me sick…"

Mia laughs. "I knew that Isa's warrior side would come out sooner or later."

"There is no warrior side."

"Oh, there is. And I can't wait to see it when she finally unleashes vengeance on all who have done her wrong!" I can only shake my head.

"Any news on that eye candy you've been looking at for years now?" I groan. "Come on, Iz, he was all over you last week." I raise my eyebrows at her choice of words. "So I'm sure he'll want to ask you for, I don't know, last-minute teaching tips or maybe a little something something." She winks. The near kiss flashes before my eyes again, forcing me to smile. "So there is a little something going on…" She grins.

"Stop being so crude." I shake my head. "Besides, remember he has a girlfriend."

"I wouldn't trust anything that comes out of that tramp's filthy mouth," she snarls. "She is an attention whore. I know there are influencers out there that work hard and do good works, Mr. Beast, for example." I nod. "But she's a spoiled brat who does nothing. She just doesn't want to work!" My bestie is not entirely wrong.

"I guess you're right."

"Of course, I'm right. That's why I'm your best friend!"

CHAPTER 11

For these first couple weeks of classes, I insist on some icebreakers and acting exercises since the textbooks I've ordered take a while to arrive. I share with them what is expected, including getting them comfortable with themselves and with one another. When they asked about the major productions and what we are doing for each class, I explain that it will be based on this year's students. I hope that will keep them at bay for while.

Soon, I have a good feel for each group. With only five classes, I can create a different syllabus for each group based on their experience and personalities. At this point, they seem to blend well, but of course, that may change as the school year continues.

Ryan pops his head in after the final class on the third Friday. "Hey, you have plans for tonight?"

Oh my gosh, is he going to ask me on a date? Wait, he has a girlfriend or someone claiming to be his girlfriend? I try to maintain a straight face, "The game."

"The game?" He looks confused for the moment. "Oh, the American football game." He enters and sinks into one of the more giant bean bags I have lying around in the classroom.

I smirk. "Well, yeah, I guess, but we just call it football…"

His hand goes to the back of his neck, which is something he does quite often. "Moving back from across the pond, I have simply forgotten some of the American vernacular and traditions."

That revelation makes me realize that I don't know much about him. Aside from his amazing good looks, love for music and theater, and intelligence, I may have idealized a version of him in my head. "When did you move back?"

"I stayed four more years at Northwestern before heading back to the UK." He studies my face. "Oh, you meant, when did I return stateside... about a month ago."

"Wow, whirlwind," I comment.

He chuckles, "I suppose." He wiggles around on the bean bag. "These are quite comfortable."

"Yeah, but it can get difficult to get up from."

Ryan struggles a bit. "I'm feeling that. Hand, please."

I laugh as I approach. I reach out and brace myself to prevent him from pulling me down. He grabs my hand and pulls himself up, bringing himself close to my body, his face once again near mine. I breathe his woodsy essence in and take a step back before we are in the same position as we were before.

He looks deflated. "Thank you."

I just nod. "I have to go home and get ready."

"Are you a super fan with the school color makeup and the works?" He snickers.

"No… not going that far. But it does get a bit chilly as the sun sets." I pause. "Plus I have to pick up Mia."

"Does she not have transportation?"

"She does, but you and I and the staff get premium parking near the stadium, so she takes advantage of that."

He laughs. "Right. I could escort both of you if you wish."

I bite my lip. "I don't think Wesley would be too thrilled with that."

"Wesley?"

"Her significant other. They're high school sweethearts."

I hear a sigh of relief, or I imagine I did. "Impressive," he comments. "Well, I can walk back with you to our humble abode if you so wish."

I am about to respond when Kim Jensen knocks on the door. "Miss Macayo? I was wondering…" She enters and sees Ryan and me. "Oh, I'm not interrupting, am I?"

"No," we say in unison.

Her eyes dart back and forth between the two of us, and a smile forms on her face.

"Miss Jensen?" Ryan prompts.

It takes her a moment to gather her thoughts, which by then has her grinning like Wonderland's Cheshire Cat. "Actually, Mr. Marks, you were the one I was looking for."

Oh? It has something to do with choir. Ryan's face is as confused as I am. "I actually need to get going," I smile.

"Mr. Marks, could you please, um… lock the door when you are done? I'll see you later, Kim!" I rush to the office.

"Save me a seat at the game," He calls after me. I nod, locking up the office and exiting with my personal items backstage.

• • •

Mia and Wesley meet me at the apartment building entrance, and together we head to a restaurant in the other town for dinner. I'm still a bit perturbed by interrupting their private time a few weeks ago, plus all the Ryan moments, so my comfort level is slightly off-edge.

"Isa," Mia snaps a finger in front of my face. "Snap out of it."

"Huh?" I look at her, puzzled.

"She wants you back on planet earth," Wesley says, grabbing some fries off his girlfriend's plate, and she swats his hand right away.

"A lot is going on," I respond.

"That's been your excuse for the past month," she retorts. "Seriously, what's going on with you?"

"It's not an excuse! A new curriculum is not always easily grasped!"

"On a subject that you live and breathe," she points out.

"She's been distracted, baby," Wesley kisses her on the forehead and stuffs some of her fries into his mouth. He drinks his soda with a smirk.

"Speaking of… any news on that front?" Mia asks before taking a bite of her burger.

I swirl my milkshake around with my straw. "We're all adjusting to the new school year."

She swallows the bite. "Stop bluffing." She points a fry at me. "You know I know when you're hiding something. So share already," she dips it in ketchup before eating it.

"You know she'll keep at you," Wesley states.

I sip at the straw; the chocolate milkshake tastes ever so sweet in my mouth. I contemplate what else can taste so sweet. Mia's right; I have to snap out of it. "He stopped by a couple of times this week. We need to discuss the upcoming productions, but we haven't found the time to sit down and talk about it."

"So you need to set up a date," she grins.

"A work function."

"Okay, a work date with wine, dinner, music, condoms…"

"Work, remember?" I interrupt her before her insinuations are clearer. "All professional, Nothing personal."

"The two can mix," Wesley adds. "It certainly won't be the first time."

• • •

The excitement in the air is contagious especially since it's the first home game of the season. We get to the stadium and find some good seats in the alumni/staff section. Most of us are dressed in school colors and other school paraphernalia. While I'm not the biggest sports fan, I do what I can to support my students, and hopefully, in return, they'll come to see their classmates in performances. It's a win-win in my opinion. Plus, it's not like I have a life anyways.

The announcer asks the audience to stand and welcomes the advanced choir to the fifty-yard line for the national anthem. I find this odd, as it is normally a soloist or a smaller group performing this patriotic act. But there they are, led by Ryan Marks himself. How did he forget this game, or did he need me to do him a favor? That's probably all it was; he wanted me to feed his cat or fish. That's all. I shouldn't have assumed.

After a quick look at the group, I notice one missing person I know would've taken this class. I guess that's why Kim came by earlier to tell him that she wouldn't make it. On the other hand, Bryce is here, but I can tell his performance has no passion.

On the other hand, their choir leader is having the time of his life. Ryan is enjoying this leadership role and is very proud of their performance. I may be biased, but this is the best the choir has sounded in years. Once they end with a flourish, the crowd literally goes wild (I know the phrase has been overused, but there is no other way to describe it), and the teacher encourages them to bow to their adoring audience. The singers are genuinely pleased and give each other hugs and high-fives. Ryan looks up at the stands, and I swear he looks right at me.

Mia gives me a sideways glance. "Yeah, I don't think that he wants to keep things professional." I roll my eyes, but my heart is pounding a mile a minute.

• • •

Kickoff starts quickly, and the choir kids join the student section. Ryan wanders in front of the bleachers, looking… well, I'm hoping for me. Mia sees him and waves her arms widely. His eyes meet mine, and he begins to go up the stands.

"Hey," he grins. "Mia, right?" He reaches over me to give her a handshake. "And you…"

Wesley offers his hand. "Wes, Mia's other half aside from Isa there."

"Ryan." The guys shake hands.

"Nice to finally meet you. The girls talk a lot about you, Isa particularly." I glare at him in shock, and Wes winks at me playfully. Mia smacks him with the back of her hand but has a big grin. I'm going to die.

"Well, all good things I hope," Ryan chuckles. He looks around the section before we all sit down during a timeout. "I see that this sport is still at an all-time high."

"You'll never get rid of football," I respond. "It's a pastime. And as American as apple pie." Wow, that's cheesy.

He makes his hand-to-neck move. "I guess I never really understood the game while I was a student here in America. My mates played of course, both here and at uni."

We rise with the crowd for a first and five for our team. We cheer to encourage them. Ryan shares the enthusiasm, despite not fully understanding what is happening.

"Well, you should drop by sometimes. There are pro games on Thursdays, Sundays, and Mondays, and of course, there's college ball on Saturdays. And Fridays are for our high school teams," Wesley offers before the crowd stands and screams again. Wellingworth's play pays off, as the receiver catches the ball and runs it seventeen yards.

"First and ten!" Mia screams. "Just a few more yards, boys!"

"I may have to take you up on your offer." Ryan laughs upon seeing Mia's reaction to the last play. "It seems you know a lot about the sport."

"Touchdown, Wellingworth," the announcer screams. And we all celebrate as the fireworks go off.

"Wow," he says amused, as we all finally sit down.

"Wow?" I ask.

"All this for a high school American football game? It seems a lot but enjoyable." He smiles at me, and I return it briefly before putting my head down, feeling my face turn red.

"It's an open invitation, man," Wesley reiterated, watching the kickoff for the away team.

"Isa could give you a ride," Mia suggests as she slides closer to her boyfriend.

"You cold, baby?" Without waiting for a response, Wesley wraps his arm around her. I swear these two will be the end of me with all these suggestions and hint-dropping.

I sit frozen, trying not to draw attention. Ryan looks over to me, "If you're cold, I can give you my jacket, Isa. Just ask."

"Thanks," I mumble. I look at the student section and see Bryce slink away with urgency. First, Kim's visit this afternoon and no show, and now this, I have to make sure my students are okay.

I excuse myself to get by Ryan. He stands and asks if all is okay, and all I can tell him is I don't know. He then joins me as I carefully walk down the bleachers, feeling if I go too fast, I will face plant. Ryan supports me via my elbow, and we get through the crowd together.

I search for Bryce near concessions and find him heading out the exit. "Bryce!" I call out. He doesn't hear me.

"Mr. Billings!" Ryan shouts, and that makes the student freeze like he's caught doing something inappropriate. We catch up to him.

"Oh hey, Miss M. Mr. Marks," the teen says. "Is everything okay?"

"That's what I was going to ask you," I state. "Where's Kim?"

"She wasn't feeling well, so I was going to visit her in the dorms," Bryce blushes.

"Are you in a rush to see her?" My fellow instructor asks.

"Of course…."

"But?" I ask.

"Come on, Miss M, everything is good."

"I'm not buying this copacetic thing. What's going on?" The student stays silent. I look at Ryan. "Did she tell you why she wasn't going to be here tonight?"

The man nods his head. "She said she is under the weather and wasn't going to make it tonight. I assume nothing unusual for teenagers."

So close to the beginning of the school year? "Can I go, please?" Bryce asks, breaking my train of thought. "I'll have her talk to you as soon as possible, Miss M. Promise."

My eyebrows rise. Something is going on. I pinch the bridge of my nose. "Yes."

"Good night!" He runs off toward the dormitories.

"Did we just let him go to shag his girlfriend?" Ryan chuckles.

I shake my head. "I don't think so. There was a sense of panic in his voice. Something's off."

CHAPTER 12

My voice is a little hoarse after last night's game. It's a tally in the Wellingworth win column, but we face Wesley's alma mater next week, which is always a powerhouse of athleticism, so it will be a tense week for everyone.

I begin to prepare for the day, shower, breakfast, etc. My phone buzzes. It's Ryan.

> hey

Suddenly I'm picturing the Ryan Gosling Hey Girl memes. I giggle before responding back.

> Good morning to you, too!
>
> actually its afternoon

What?! I stare at the microwave clock, and it's 10:30. Yes, I sleep in on weekends but never that late.

> Funny. Thanks for giving me a heart attack.
>
> do you need me to resuscitate you?

The idea of mouth-to-mouth with my high school crush perks me up. I know if I cross that line, I'll never be able to take it back, and if it doesn't work out, the heartache it will cause would be so great. I don't need that in my life right now.

> Fully recovered. Thanks.
> free 2day for a prod mtg?

Stay aloof, Isa. Don't show that you don't have a life.

> Sure.

> 6 my place
> need directions?
> i'll make dinner

I smirk. But if dinner is involved, things can go in a totally different direction.

> How about the cafe at 2:00 pm?

He takes a bit to respond. Am I making him change his plans for today? Does he have an afternoon date?

> ill c u then

• • •

I change to something more appropriate for a meeting, and at 1:45, head downstairs with my laptop. I could stake a good table and look professional. Passing by his door, I am tempted to see if he was still in his apartment, and I think better of it and go through the employee back entrance of the cafe. The staff greets me, and I smile as I look around for a place to camp. I freeze when I saw him at one of the tables already… with Zoey Waines.

My heart drops. Well, it's a good thing I wanted to keep this professional, right?

"Isa?" The barista gets my attention. I turn around and thank them for my drink. I look for a table in an attempt to stay invisible, which of course, is impossible once my name is announced.

Ryan stands and smiles with a gesture to take the chair across from him. Zoey scowls, sending my daggers my way.

I step over there. "Am I interrupting?"

"Yes," Zoey growls. Ryan rolls his eyes, or at least I think he does. His expression is sweet just a split second later.

"Don't be a ninny." Ouch. "Please sit."

"Really, I don't want to impose."

"We have a meeting," he insists.

Zoey puts her hand on his arm, fingering his muscles. "Awww… but Ry-Ry," she whines. "We just started settling in. Surely this meeting can wait till Monday."

"The one-act show's audition is in a fortnight…"

"What does the game have to do with this?" The 23-year-old asks very confusedly.

"He means…"

She nearly bites my head off. "I know what he means, Eye-za. Whatever kind of name that is. I was joking."

I huff. I am not in the mood for this. "Mr. Marks, I have the fall show under control. Once I have that going, I'll contact you about the winter showcase and spring musical. Hope you enjoy your day!" I flash my teeth in a gritted smile before heading out.

"Isa, wait…" Without looking back, I hear a bit of a commotion, but I simply continue back to the residences. Ryan never follows.

CHAPTER 13

The preparations for the fall show are in full swing. I have a volunteer tech crew working on a very minimal set, easy enough to transition to three different scenes with little effort. (Note to self: Add a tech course next year). Audition slots are filling up quickly. My classes are going well; the acting groups are encouraging one another and shelling out good advice for the auditions.

The Tuesday before the auditions, I am going over the audition list during my advanced acting class, when I notice two regular names missing, Bryce Billings and Kim Jensen. I frown; normally they're the first ones to sign up. I ask Tori Ann Childs, Kim's roommate and best friend, to my office.

"Is everything okay, Miss Macayo?" The teenager asks.

I casually sit on the other edge of my desk. "You're doing great, sweetie," I start delicately. I don't want to seem like I have favorites, but as a staple in our school productions, all three of these kids have always been involved. "I look forward to your audition. You'll have to be one of our leaders out there."

Tori Ann beams. "Thank you." She studies my face for a moment and thoughtfully adds, "But you want to know about Kimbers, don't you?"

I sigh. "Well, yes… It seems she's been distracted a lot lately, and when she is here she slips out of class a lot.

That's not like her. I know as her roommate you can't tell me what it is, but if there's something I can do to help."

She purses her lips and thinks long and hard before speaking. "You have been and are and always will be our favorite teacher, Miss Macayo. Really. Especially after you picked me from that one unfortunate incident last year…" I hold my finger up and shake my head, not wanting her to bring it up again. "But as you said, it's not my place to say. I know I brought it up a few times to talk to you. Bryce did the same thing. I just don't think she's ready yet."

Oh my gosh. Something is wrong. I don't want to pry, but I want to make it right. I simply nod. "Okay, then. Please let her know that I'm here when she needs me, and you all can always message me if need be."

"We know," she says with a smile. "You're the best."

"Thanks. Now…"

She stands up and walks back to the classroom. "I know."

• • •

Thursday comes around, and I'm proud of the preparation my classes have done. My advanced class even did an open workshop for other students who aren't in my classes but are interested in auditioning.

After school, I put a binder and water bottle on the best seat in the house, right smack in the middle of the auditorium. I truly believe the architects stood on this spot and ensured the acoustics and view are perfect.

There is still an hour before the first audition, which is allotted to give the kids time to go back to their dorms or home, change to more comfortable clothes, grab a snack, etc. I go to my office to grab a granola bar for myself when Ryan comes by with two cups of coffee from the cafe and a small bag, which smells a lot like a warm cheese danish.

"I'm glad to catch you," he hands me one of the cups. I breathe it in; it's my typical order, caramel macchiato.

"Thanks," I mumble, taking a soothing sip.

He grins. "I'm hoping to finesse my way to helping you with auditions."

I raise my eyebrows. "Oh?"

He dangles the pastry bag in front of me; the warm smell is intoxicating. "I imagine whatever's in here is better than that granola bar."

"I suppose it is," I respond.

"So would you be willing to consider letting me help with this production in exchange for this delicious pastry?" His eyebrows waggle.

I look at him delicately. Would I want to spend more time with him? Of course, no doubt in my mind. A million times, yes. Would it be professional? It has to be. Do I want it to cross the line? There lies the problem. Plus, doesn't he have a girlfriend? I mean, Zoey clings onto him anytime they're together.

"Are you considering it?" There's his sexy easy-going smile that makes my insides melt.

I try to stay aloof. "I probably could use a hand for the show, but I'm not sure if it's worth one cheese danish."

He moves in closer, dipping his head so he can whisper, "I'll make it worth your while." I shiver slightly and almost moan. Instead, I gulp and do my best to make stay composed.

A knock comes at the door. He jumps back quickly. Kim and Bryce are at the door. The teen boy has a smirk on his face, and Kim is red in the face to prevent herself from giggling.

"Right, I'll be back in fifteen minutes to help with auditions," Ryan says. "Miss Jensen, Mr. Billings," he almost leaves but turns around and gives me the danish. "No food in the auditorium, right?" And with that, he walks away.

I take a moment to gather myself before looking at the teen couple. "My timing is never good, is it?" Kim asks as she bursts into a fit of giggles.

"You might need to adjust the temperature in here, Miss M." Bryce chuckles.

I shake my head and nod toward the loveseat. "Sit please."

They do and take a minute to calm down. I lean back on my desk, facing them. "If you guys are asking to make it to see if there are additional spots for today, I'm afraid there aren't. We're full, which is surprising for the fall show."

The couple looks at each other before shaking their heads. "Can I please close the doors?" Bryce asks and does so before I can respond. He sits back down and grabs his girlfriend's hand.

"Tori Ann says you were concerned about me," Kim begins, looking at Bryce for courage. He nods. "I know you and Mr. Marks were making sure we're okay at the first home game."

"Well, I must admit I find it disconcerting when two of our main players aren't offering to be in this show."

"I'm going to miss this show!" Kim bursts into tears, and Bryce reaches out to her, enveloping her in his arm, and comforting her.

After a moment, she calms down enough to blurt out the words, "I'm pregnant!" I do everything in my power not to gasp aloud. I know students aren't exactly chaste here, but I thought they'd be more responsible than not using protection.

"We're nearly sixteen weeks along," Bryce informs me.

That detail makes me react. She's four months along, and it's early October, which means, she got pregnant at the end of last school year. "When did you find out?"

"The day we were moving out for the summer," she says. "I didn't go home. I told my parents that I got an internship in town, not like they would check on it. They were ready to go spend the summer in Europe, so I didn't feel so bad."

"She stayed with me," Bryce adds. "I snuck her into the apartment every night for a week before my mom says that it was stupid that I was hiding her. She says she knew that Kim was there the whole time."

"We weren't sure what we wanted to do with the baby. We were juggling with the idea of abortion," Kim scrunches her face, and Bryce shakes his head and comforts her again. "But once we heard the heartbeat, there was no chance in hell we were going to do that. And it may be selfish, but we want to finish school."

"That's not selfish at all," I reply.

"It is when you're thinking about how to finish in a private school versus going to a public school," Kim says sadly.

"It's what you're familiar with," I attempt to ease her concerns.

"Plus what do we know about taking care of a baby?!" This time she really begins crying, and Bryce squeezes her more.

"Many people who are less mature than you are having babies every day. You being here, confiding in me, and letting me know your concerns, shows so much responsibility and caring for this child. This child will be blessed no matter what."

"That's the thing, Miss M," Bryce starts. "I don't want to do that to my mom. She had a hard enough time raising me by herself, she can't do this all over again."

"What about Kim's parents?" The question tumbles out of my mouth, but I soon regret asking it, knowing the answer.

Kim snorts. "They'll want me to get a late-term abortion or send me further away to have the baby. It'll be bad for their image."

"Plus they're not exactly fond of me," the teen boy wistfully adds. "I'm not what they think their daughter deserves."

"Which is bullshit," Kim says angrily.

"Kimberly!"

"Sorry, Miss Macayo, but seriously Bryce is perfect for me. I love him," she turns to him. "I love you so much." He brushes her hair out of the way and kisses her on the forehead, mumbling something only she could hear. I smile.

"So the only conclusion we came up with is to put him or her up for adoption," Bryce finishes softly.

"We want him or her to have a good home with loving parents," Kim says.

"We'll love him or her no matter what, but we want to do what's best for all of us," he continues.

"I'm very impressed at your action plan," I remark.

"We were actually hoping…" Kim starts but blushes, placing her face into her boyfriend's shoulder.

"If you and Mr. Marks would adopt the baby," Bryce concludes.

I am taken aback. What?! "Mr. Marks and I aren't together."

"Or at least you," he continues. "You are phenomenal with us teenagers, and we're sure you'll give this baby a lot of love."

My mind is going a mile a minute. "Are you sure you want the baby to be raised where you could see him or her? Wouldn't you just want to grant temporary custody to someone?"

They both shake their head. "For the baby's sake, consistency will be best," Bryce says.

"So you'll do it?" Kim asks hopefully.

I want to say yes. I want to make sure their futures as well as their child's future are good. But I'm a single thirty-something living in a single-bedroom apartment with no prospective partner in sight. What kind of life will I be able to give this child? I know single parents can handle it; look at Bryce's mom, who worked three jobs just to make sure they have food on the table and a roof over their heads. But do I have that type of resilience? I know my family will go ape if I have a child out of wedlock and tell me there's no way I can handle it without a husband or, just like Kim's parents, express how it will affect their reputation with their community. Too much to consider.

"I need time to think about it. It's a lot to take in," I say cautiously. They nod solemnly. "I'm not ruling it out completely, but there's a lot to consider."

"We understand," Bryce says.

"Thank you for at least listening to us about it," Kim says.

They get up, and I give them a group hug. "Hey, I didn't say no. Just let me think about it for a bit."

"We know, Miss M."

CHAPTER 14

I walk from the stage to the auditorium in a complete daze. I'm not even sure how I got to my seat; when Ryan sat next to me or was he there before I got there?

"Are you okay, love?"

I didn't answer right away. How am I supposed to answer that question? No, two of our students are having a baby, and they want us to adopt him. Laugh and tell him the students think we're together and want us to raise their love child. Or I'm in love with you; let's get married and adopt Kim and Bryce's baby? Or better yet, there's a good chance I'm getting a baby in five months.

No, none of those work because I don't know what to do. I know that I have to keep it a secret for Kim and Bryce's sake, even though she'll be showing soon at four months, and who knows how quickly that will spread around campus.

"How was the danish?" Ryan asks, trying to get me out of my funk.

Danish? The Danish! "Oh, um…. I left it in the office, and I didn't have time to eat it. I appreciate you bringing it, though."

"Well, I guess bribing my way to helping you with this show works," he laughs and moves closer to me. "Don't worry, I won't tell the kids it's that easy to get to you."

When I don't react like I normally do, he looks puzzled. "Isa, what's wrong, baby?"

Baby? I shake my head. "Just got a lot on my mind, that's all."

"I can see that. What can I do to make it better?" He reaches for my hand and traces the back of it with his fingers. I pull away quickly.

He clears his throat. "Right, in all seriousness, I'm glad I can help you with this."

"You didn't give me much of a choice," I reply.

"Do you think that I planned on being interrupted by the students?"

"I never said that."

"I told you when the school year began that I can be of assistance to you. I know theater as well as I know vocal performance."

"I know that as well."

"Then what is it?"

"Really, Ryan? I…. I…. " I was in love with you decades ago, and now that you're back those feelings resurfaced. "I think we should just keep it professional. I mean, I don't want to give them the impression that we're together."

He opens his mouth as if to say something but closes it after a heartbeat. He simply nods. I see a hint of disappointment in his eyes, but that could just be me hoping.

• • •

This first wave of auditions goes exceptionally well. Despite all my distractions, including the one sitting next to me, I am able to concentrate on what type of actors are needed for each act. I occasionally peek at Ryan's notes to see if he has the same thought patterns as I do, but as the director, I have the final say.

After the last student finishes with their monologue and the house lights turn on, I rub my temples to focus on this first round of cuts. There are a lot of good thespians to choose from, and I hate to admit it, but some aren't even in my classes (yet).

Ryan clears his throat. I feel some disconnection between the two of us after I told him to keep it professional. It's only been a couple of hours, and already I hate it. "There are a lot of talent to choose from."

"It's not going to be easy."

"Er… how do you want me to share these notes with you? Callbacks are tomorrow, right?"

I nod. "I guess you can email me who you think deserves to get called back, and I'll see if it matches my list."

He thinks for a moment. "I'll have to you by ten. Would that be too late?" I shake my head. "Right."

"Thank you for doing this with me," I sincerely say to him with a small smile.

He gives a curt nod. "Good night, Miss Macayo." Before I can respond, he takes his stuff and leaves me alone with just my thoughts.

• • •

It turns out Ryan and I have similar thoughts about who should go forward, with the exception of five people. I email those who called back and invite those who didn't to get additional experience with tech and crew. I make sure my fellow teacher, Mr. Marks, was cc'd on all communique.

If he is such a distraction to everything I have to sort through, why is my heart hurting right now that I'm keeping him at a distance?

CHAPTER 15

Production rehearsal is in full swing. I recruit Kim to be the assistant student director to Ryan and myself, knowing she would be happy to have a part in the show. What I wasn't expecting is her very emotional response to the invite. We also give Bryce the stage manager spot.

Although I still haven't given a response to their inquiry about adoption, I'm glad they know I can help them out. Kim and Bryce invited me to the gender reveal ultrasound (it's a girl), and I make sure that Kim stays healthy for both of their sakes.

And as expected, her pregnancy is the best-known secret all over campus. While this may be shocking for these groups of students, I know it's been known to happen once in a while and has ended in different ways, depending on their support or lack of support. Goodness, I know a story about a former student's water breaking in the middle of class and with contractions, and she still insisted on staying until that particular class was over. Dedication right there.

But of course, not everyone would be supportive. Some will frown upon what Kim and Bryce have decided or spread horrible lies about them. Thankfully his mom, even though she's not on campus, Tori Ann, and several staff members, including Ryan Marks, have their backs and will support them through this.

Ryan. He's the other person that's been on my mind more than before. I thought that by keeping things professional, I would be able to not worry about him. I should have taken cues from romantic comedies and romance novels that the opposite of what you really want never works. It makes things more awkward, especially since we work so often together. Gosh, darn it to pieces. Or maybe I'm over-analyzing things again. I mean, I hear Zoey is gleefully coming over to the choir classroom more often. So maybe I'm (ruefully) speeding up what's supposed to be happening between them.

• • •

Roughly two weeks before opening night, we are trying to smooth out a few kinks in the show, whether it is props, set changes, or the acting. Kim asks to return to the dorms because her feet hurt, and she has a paper due the following day. So it is just Ryan, stage manager Bryce and I trying to get through the second one act. This was a romantic comedy scene, and our two leads, Jordy and Willa, have difficulty portraying that "in love" feeling leading to their kiss, which hasn't been practiced yet. Ryan and I have spoken to the respective students (Ryan to Jordy, I to Willa) about what they can do to exude this, but nothing is catching. At this point, after almost four weeks of rehearsals, I almost want to ask the understudies to take over. And anytime I ask for his input, Ryan simply shrugs and says, "you're the director; it's your call." Thanks, assistant director.

However, when I ask the understudies if they would be ready to take over if necessary, their eyes show pure panic. They are two freshmen who probably never wanted to be leads in a play so soon.

I look at Ryan once more before groaning and dipping (wanting to pound) my head on the backrest of the seat in front of me. He sighs, "I'll see what I can do," before going up on stage to talk to the two teenagers.

I guess I can still cancel this one and just make it two one-acts.

"Miss Macayo, can you please come to the stage?" Ryan asks impatiently. Oh boy. What is happening that manages to get this usually easy-going guy irate? Then again, he's been irate since he asked to help out with the production a month ago.

As I go up the stairs to the stage, the two leads go down to the seats. I glare at Ryan. "What's going on?"

"Apparently," he begins curtly, "We need to demonstrate how this is going to be done because they are saying it's better to lead by example."

I glare at the four teenagers, both the two leads and the understudies. "Seriously, guys? We gave you many hints and asked you to watch rom-coms to get the picture."

"Yeah, but the stage is a whole different atmosphere," Willa says innocently. I narrow my eyes at her. "You always say that there are bigger gestures than on film because we have to reach the back of the room."

Ryan smirks. "You do say that." I give him the stink eye.

"And apparently we've tried multiple times using your suggestions," Jordy replies. "So maybe you and Mr. Marks can just show us how this needs to go, maybe we'll just copy you two."

I close my eyes. Are you kidding me?! I have to show them how to portray a woman in love and share a kiss. With my high school crush, my current infatuation, and the man I'm doing my best to keep a more professional relationship because I don't need another thing to worry about and I don't want to get my heart broken. Simple task, right?

"We're both professionals," Ryan's eyes find mine for the first time in a month. There is a sense of something there, but I can't place it.

I gulp. "Yeah, okay," I ask one of the kids for the book.

Ryan reads as the lead male character. "There are too many forces going against us, Bonnie. I want this to work, but…"

I become the lead female. "But what, Daniel? Is it too much to ask for everything? I guess it is. Happiness doesn't allow us to have everything, right?"

His gaze glares into my soul. I don't know if he's playing a role now or being himself. His stare is so deep.

"It is worth fighting for. You're worth fighting for." He steps closer to me. "Tell me you don't want to be with me."

"I can't do that." My eyes stay on his, not wanting to blink. Is it me that doesn't want to blink or my character? I don't know if I'm holding my breath for emphasis or because I want this moment as Ryan and myself.

Using his upstage hand, he cups my face gently; the other hand, still holding a copy of the script, is on the small of my back. Something about his touch exudes more than the playwright intended. "Then let's fight it," he says in a stage whisper. He pulls me close and takes a moment to search my eyes even more. His gaze communicates that he needs this to happen, but I'm not sure if it's from Ryan or from the character he's portraying.

I close my eyes as our lips press together in a gentle kiss. However, our connection urges me to go beyond the stage kiss that I want to show the students. This kiss is slowly becoming our kiss. The kiss that has been interrupted multiple times since he showed up in my apartment building. This kiss is everything I've ever wanted, I've needed, and I've feared. I drop the script and wrap my arms over his shoulders. My hands massage his neck. His grip on me tightens as he tilts his head slightly to deepen the kiss.

"Ahem!" Bryce clears his throat from the wing. We pull away from each other, breathing heavily. Our eyes lock, and I gulp. Neither of us knows what to say to each other or the students.

"And that is how it's done," Bryce says, humor in his voice. "Any questions?" I bite my lower lip, trying to regain composure.

"So if we perform this like seven minutes in heaven?" Jordy asks with a grin.

"No!" Both Ryan and I exclaim simultaneously.

"So, more like just making out?" The teen tries again, and Willa jabs him with her elbow.

"Um… maybe that's enough for tonight," I announce. "You both have my class tomorrow; we can discuss it then." Then looking at the understudies. "We'll also talk about it in a few days."

The students nod, smirking at one another before pouncing up the stage to get their stuff. I turn to our stage manager. "So I'm done too? I'm going to check on Kim before heading home," He is grinning from ear to ear.

Ryan is in the back of the house; he looks up at me. I am still speechless. He gives me this look of longing, or what I interpret as wanting. I close my eyes. That kiss is from me, not a character or a role. Is it the same for him? I open my eyes, and he is gone.

CHAPTER 16

The rumor mill is in full swing. As I work with Willa and Jordy, the rest of the class whispers loudly about Ryan and me. I turn to them and clear my throat. They all look at me, most with knowing smiles. "Don't you have an assignment due today?" Most of them groan. "I'm positive it's due today… or we can move the deadline up to the end of class." Some shake their heads. "It's your choice."

Scott Webber, a senior actor in the comedic one-act, raises his hand but asks his question without my acknowledgment. "Miss Macayo, are we adding firefighters to the second act because I heard there's a smoldering fire!" Some of the other boys laugh and high-five one another: Jordy snickers, eyebrows waggling at Willa, who smacks him in the chest to make him stop.

I smile, "I'll tell you what, Scott, just for that, you'll have to recite your original monologue five minutes before the end of class." The senior looks at me in shock, and his friends look down at their desks. "Anyone else want to share theirs as well?" Everyone else shakes their head. "Get to work."

I turn to my two leads to ask what looks like will work for them. "Tongue, definitely tongue," Jordy replies without hesitation. Willa scrunches her face and shakes her head defiantly.

"Not the kiss, the dialogue be-" Suddenly, the classroom door swings open, and Zoey stomps into the room. "Excuse me," I cry. "I'm in the middle of cla-" Her open palm is in the air, about to connect with my face, when Jordy grabs her arm, pushing it back to her side. The class gasps in unison, watching this unfold from their desks.

"Don't touch me," she snarls at the teen boy. Her breath reeks of alcohol, and both students recoil in disgust. She turns to me and wags a finger to my face, "And you, keep your hands off Ryan Marks. He's mine!"

I take deep breaths to take control of the situation. "Miss Waines, as I was about to say earlier, I have a class at the moment." I wave at the students. Some of whom are sneering at her. Some guys are ogling at her minimum amount of clothing. The rest watches their mouth agape. "I do recommend you rest up, and we can have a discussion with the headmaster during my planning period later today."

"Isn't it against school policy to have alcohol around minors?" Willa adds icily.

"You're going to pay," she threatens. "Stay away from him."

"He's the assistant director of the show, kinda hard to keep him away from her," Scott smirks. I look over at him and shake my head, not wanting to add more ammunition to this nonsense.

"Go back to your room and rest," I repeat.

"She's saving your ass, bitch," Jordy says under his breath.

Zoey screams in frustration and stomps away, slamming my door behind her. The class exhales collectively, and I pinch the bridge of my nose and give instructions evenly. "Please return to working on your monologues."

• • •

"The harlot did what?!" Mia exclaims as I call her during lunch. "I can't believe she had the audacity to do that. What triggered it anyways?"

"Rumors," I reply before taking a bite of my sandwich.

"Must be some pretty heavy stuff to trigger a drunken outrage." A knock sounds from my office door. Ryan stands there, his hazel eyes filled with concern. "Um… Mi, I gotta go. I'll text you tonight." I hang up without another word. "Hi."

"I can return if this is a bad time."

"I just hung up the phone. I can talk." About what is the question.

He stays at the doorway, massaging his neck. "My students have nothing on The Sun," Curiously, I look for clarity. "The tabloid?" I simply nod, not knowing where he is headed with this conversation. "It seems that you and I had a perform lewd sex act on this very stage last night," he says with his easy-going smile. I choke on my drinking water. So much for professionalism.

"What?!" I squeak out.

"Exaggerations," he says, amused.

"Please tell me you corrected them."

"Did you correct your students? As I'm sure, we have several of the same students today."

"Willa and Jordy were working on the scene before your favorite eye candy barged into my class." He is bewildered. "Zoey was drunk and was ready to fight me for you."

Ryan's shocked face says a lot but not all the information that I needed. "Are you all right?"

I shrug. "Jordy grabbed her arm before she could lay a finger on me." Ryan exhales in relief. "There's something wrong with that girl."

He seems to have nodded, but his expression is hard to read. When he doesn't say anything, I grab a Cool Ranch Doritos snack bag from my desk. He eyes the bag, looking as if he wants to take it from me. For some odd reason, I use this opportunity to bring the focus back to us as friends, not colleagues. Plus, I'll avoid getting heartbroken when he doesn't respond about his relationship with Zoey. "No…" I stare at him, open the bag, and take out a single chip. Then without a second thought, I flirt and stare directly into his eyes seductively. "Is this what you want?" I lick the chip with a slight grin before taking a nibble.

He groans. "Now, who's not being professional."

I open my bottom drawer, and after searching through the variety box, I find another Cool Ranch and throw it at him. "Don't you ever bring your own lunch?"

"Well, now I know where your secret stash of snacks is, no." He opens the bag and chops on a large chip.

"If I find out that you took the last of my favorite chips, I will hunt you down," I glare at him. He keeps eating chips, returning my glare with a smile. "I have a very particular set of skills. Skills I have acquired over a very long career. Skills that make me a nightmare for people like you."

He laughs. "I don't believe that's the line!"

"It is so," I giggle.

"Okay, so Cool Ranch Doritos and Dr. Pepper," he says.

"How did you know about Dr. Pepper?"

"You and Mia always have it for your girl nights."

"Creep," I grin.

He takes the last chip out of his bag. "These are small bags." He throws out the bag and wipes his hands on his pants. "Rehearsals tonight?"

"Be there or be square."

"What does that even mean?"

"I have no clue."

CHAPTER 17

The performance weekend finally arrives. We run through the final dress rehearsal. The first one act, the drama, is flawless with one minor prop omission. The actors cover the mistake, and Scott and the comedic one-act have their timing down pat. There are a few times when I wish they would slow down and wait for the reaction, but nothing that will affect the show badly.

Our romantic comedy one-act is much better than it was two weeks ago. However, the kiss needs a bit of improvement.

"Willa, you must stop laughing when he gets near you!" I call out from the middle of the auditorium.

"I told you we need to do it with tongue," Jordy recommends, wagging his tongue.

"Gag me," Willa pretends to do so.

"And we told you, you don't have to do it exactly how we showed you a fortnight ago." Ryan quips. My face turns red. He and I never bring up the kiss, except as an example for the show during rehearsals. Thankfully the student's reaction brings us back from the awkwardness we experienced when we kept it "professional."

"I don't think ANYONE can match that, Mr. Marks," Bryce yells from the wing. "Well, maybe Kim and I…" He winks at his girlfriend.

"Yeah, and the bun in the oven proves it!" Scott shouts back. If the cast and crew didn't know about her pregnancy, they do now.

"Hey!" I clap my hands, and the students clap back right away. I love the conditioning they learn from elementary school. "Wasting time here. The pacing and acting are good... until that point. We need to find a solution tonight. What can we do to stop the giggles."

The cast and crew are actually silently considering different options.

"How about the kiss on the cheek?" A young freshman girl quietly offers.

Ryan shakes his head. "Unfortunately, that requires them to be close to each other. I appreciate the idea!" The girl beams. I catch Ryan's eyes and smile. He's honed his teaching skills down.

"How about they hold hands," Kim thinks aloud. There are a few groans from the guys. "Wait... Hear me out! Bryce, can you get Kacey at the board to fade to dark on my cue?"

"Of course," he smiles and talks to his headset. I see Kacey at the booth give a thumbs up.

"Jordy, what's your last line before the kiss?"

"Let's fight it."

I watch Kim's face as she figures out a solution. I give Ryan a sideways glance, and he's looking at her proudly and winks at me. "Can we add the word 'together' at the end of that?"

"Can we?" Jordy agrees slowly. I nod, shrugging.

"Once you say that line, offer your hand like you're asking for her hand. Palm up," Kim directs. "Look at her with love."

"Okay…" He does as he is instructed.

"Willa," Kim turns her attention to the female lead. "Wait a beat, then flash your loving smile…" She waits until Willa smiles. "Not at me, at Jordy. And gently put your hand on his." The other teen girl does so. "Both of you freeze with those looks in your eyes. Bryce, drop lights gently." Her boyfriend talks on the headset, and the stage goes dark. Kim looks at us, her teachers, for approval.

"It might work. Bryce, lights up." I move to the center seat again. Ryan watches from a few rows near the front center. "Take it from the 'Tell me you don't want me' line," I order.

Willa and Jordy perform the final three lines with the additional word and hold hands in lieu of the kiss. Kacey immediately knew when to drop the lights.

The cast and crew applaud enthusiastically.

Ryan meets me at the back. "We'll make her a director yet." We watch the others congratulate Kim on her innovative idea.

I nod happily. "I think we're ready."

CHAPTER 18

Opening night goes smoothly. The dramatic one act had all their props. The comedic one-act lasted a little longer, with Scott milking the audience's laughter. The romantic comedy act is the one everyone is talking about at the end of the show. Ryan and I separate as the audience exits the auditorium. Mia and Wesley are the first ones to find me.

"Oh, my God!" Mia screeches, giving me the biggest hug. "You put that together?! It was perfect!"

"I had amazing people help me out," I take a quick glance at Ryan with a small smile.

"I was even impressed," Wesley gives me one of those half-bro hugs type. "And I hate theater. Is there anywhere I can get a beer?"

"This is a school," I reply.

"But we had some at the football games," he contemplates.

"Because we smuggled it in, baby," Mia whispers with a wink.

"Hey, when is that boyfriend of yours coming by to watch the football?" Wesley asks.

I bite my lip, "He's not my boyfriend. He was my assistant director for this show, but we're just friends."

Mia looks at me with a knowing smile. "Give it time. Aren't you the next two suppose to be dependent on one another for the next two shows?"

"Yeah, I guess."

"Tita Isa!" I hear two sets of feet running toward me. I freeze. My family's here? I look at Mia.

She shakes her head. "Sorry, girl, I'm taking off. Where is Wesley?" She goes off to find her other half before two sets of arms wrap themselves around each of my legs. Angela's twins, Archie and Charlotte, found me.

I genuinely smile at my niece and nephew, crouching down. "Hey, sweet peas! Did you like it?" I wrap around both of them at the same time.

"Where's the music?" Little Charlotte asks.

"Next one, sweetie," I state.

"Isn't the next one at the benefit?" Angela inquires. Now my smile freezes and becomes a fixture to greet my sister.

"Yes, it is," I respond as I rise. "Hey, Peter!" I greet my brother-in-law, who recently returned from deployment. "Welcome back!"

He nods curtly. "Luisa. I am very glad to be back."

"Where's -"

"Oh, Katherine! You would have been perfect for that role if you go to school here!" My mother's grating voice can be heard over the crowd. I close my eyes. Breathe. My mom is escorting my oldest niece over to us. "Luisa, you make sure she gets a good role when she goes to school here."

"It'll be a while, Nay."

"She be here soon. She genius just like doctor mommy and daddy." My mother smiles proudly at my sister and her spouse. Perfect.

I clear my throat. "What did you think of the show?"

"So so, lang[10]," my mom critiques. "Story is very confusing."

"It's not one play; they are three different plays, Nay," I explained. "Each act was a different story."

My mother shakes her head. "Too much. I don't understand what is going on."

"Next time," Angela states, "Just choose a dramatic play. What's so hard about that?"

As if this family reunion couldn't get better, a high-pitched voice screams, "Ryan!" I turn just in time to see Zoey wrap her skinny arms around Ryan's neck and give him a big old smooch. I turn around. This meet and greet is getting more and more perfect as the night goes on.

• • •

After resetting the stage for the next show, the cast and crew go to their dorms or home. I stay an extra bit to write out my director's notes. Before long, I realize that it is nearing midnight; I organize my desk and lock up the classroom, my office, stage, and auditorium. I am locking the building when I hear some tussling behind me. Not sure what to expect, I grab the pepper spray out of my tote.

---

[10] Filipino translation: just okay

"You're here late." I scream and jump holding the pepper spray an arm's length away. Thankfully, I do not push the button; Ryan is a bit amused and perplexed. He immediately puts his hand up in surrender. "Isa, love," he says calmly. "It's me, Ryan. Your neighbor and colleague…" I am breathing very hard at this point; he puts his hand on mine, the one holding the pepper spray, and lowers my hand.

After my air consumption and heart rate return to normal, I slap him a couple of times on his very defined chest. "Don't you ever do that again!" He mockingly withdraws and gives me a cocky grin.

"I couldn't resist. I wanted to make sure you are safe being here so late."

"By scaring the living crap out of me?! Seriously?!" I slap him silly when he finally reaches for both of my hands and pulls me close. I gulp.

"I'll make it up to you," he says into my hair. "You leave your car here, and I'll drive us home. I'll make something to eat before you head upstairs to your place, or you're free to stay in mine."

He begins rubbing his hands up and down my arms to warm me up. His face slowly starts down the path to my cheek until we are nose to nose once more. Our eyes lock. I try reading his eyes; I want to say I see desire and passion. Oh goodness, I'm hoping that's what it is.

Suddenly a light shines on us; we part and stare at the culprit, campus security. "Oy," Ryan says to them. "It's all good, mate! This is Miss Macayo, the theater teacher, and I'm Mr. Marks, choir."

"You have ID?" the security person brings their bicycle to us. We both hold up our faculty badges. He shines the flashlight on my badge, then my face, and I wince at the bright light. He also pulls the same routine with Ryan, who surprisingly takes this as a humorous turn of events.

"Do you get cold riding your bicycle around this late in the year?" My colleague asks jovially.

The officer doesn't answer his question. "You're free to go," he tells us with disappointment in his voice before riding off to look for delinquents who are sneaking out of the dorms past curfew.

Ryan whistles. "I'm betting he has a stick up his arse."

I shake my head. "I'm beat. Thanks for the offer, but I'm going to drive home and head straight to bed."

He nods. "Fair, but I insist on escorting you to the car park." My face must have a look of confusion as he continues, "It's late, and you don't want Mr. I-have-a-wedgie-in-my-bum-because-I-ride-this-bike-all-night harassing you again."

I hold back a chuckle. "Is that his name?"

"Yes, that is his real name."

We walk towards the parking lot in silence. "You know, we still have to get together soon," he says after a moment or two.

"Don't you…"

"I meant, have a meeting about the upcoming productions," he clarifies his thinking. Darn it to pieces.

"Ryan, we just finished opening night, and we still have two more shows to do. Maybe we can talk about it next week." Our arms brush, and I shiver slightly.

"Cold?" He puts his arm around my shoulders and pulls me close to him again.

"Thanks," I sigh with contentment. "We can do this because we're friends. I don't want to put you in a compromising position with your girlfriend." I unlock my car with my fob, not wanting to see his reaction. He opens the door driver's door for me and waits till I slip in, putting my tote on the passenger seat.

He leans down, using my car's door and roof as anchors. I put the key in the ignition. "One of these days, we need to talk about what happened a fortnight ago."

"We were simply showing by example," I breathe, and my heart rate soars.

He takes a loose strand of my hair and puts it behind my ear. His voice is low and throaty. "Is that what we're calling it?"

I gulp before responding. I search his eyes. "Yes…" It's not a lie; the kids requested us to show them how to perform the scene.

Now he shakes his head. "Okay. Drive safe. I'll see you at the flats soon." With that, he closes the door and taps his hand on my car as I slowly drive away. I'm not so tired anymore.

CHAPTER 19

The final two shows are more than successful. They are hits, all because these kids just grasp the directions and guidance that Ryan and I throw at them. They adjust their attitudes and actions, creating a perfect blend that transforms the auditorium into a personal bubble for each cast.

Ryan offers to "host" the cast party in his classroom since my theater studio room is the dumping ground of their personal items. After the final meet and greet, we gather there; the students are super wired, basically jumping around about the thrill of knowing the show's success. While we directors bring out the snacks, juices, and sodas from his office, I turn to him. "Are you sure you want them here? The studio is still a disaster; we can just add to it and have them clean it on Monday."

"They're fine here." He playfully nudges me with his elbow and grins. "I can easily require my choirs to do the same thing."

During the final haul for paper products, I need to get something off my chest and softly request his attention. "Ryan."

He pauses at the doorway, and his hazel eyes return to mine, absorbing all of me. His reply is equally soft. "Yes, Isa?"

"Thank you."

"For this?"

I shake my head. "Not just this, for being my friend and an amazing co-director…"

He chuckles, "Co-director? So we're partners."

"I thought that was pretty clear two weeks ago." He raises one eyebrow. "Not just because of that…. I mean, we were…."

"Isa," he balances all he carries to one arm and reaches out to me with the other. His finger traces down my arm. "I understand."

"I'm so glad you're my friend." Why do I keep reiterating that? I know full well that I want more than friendship. "You made our first full production such as success."

"That was mostly you and them. I was just here for support."

"You're a big part of all this" We take a moment to simply look at each other, not trying to break wordless communication.

"Hey, Mr. and Miss Ms" Scott's loud voice shatters whatever is occurring between us. "Do I need a plate, or can I just dig in?" My eyes go wide, and we both scramble out there to provide essential products.

• • •

After the teens have their fill of sugary sweets and salty treats, I give my thank you speech for all their hard work and how proud I am of them. Kim and Bryce present each cast and crew member with their paper plate awards. Many of the awards are silly to match the personality of the individual. But then they turn serious, which I initially thought was a build-up for another joke. Kim allows a few tears to flow down her cheek and nods at her boyfriend. Bryce clears his throat, "And of course, these two final plates are the most accurately labeled award. All because I know we are all in agreement with this, at least, I'm pretty sure we all are," He looks around for support.

"Spit it out, Billings! How can I agree if I don't know what the hell you are talking about!" Scott shouts.

"These are the theater Mom and Dad awards," the junior smiles emotionally. Surprisingly no dissent, just more murmur from the other students

"Family doesn't mean blood relations," Willa adds.

"We are crazy," Jordy says.

Lighting queen Kacey grins. "And there's no one else more that I would consider family on top of my biologically related fools than all these idiots."

"Thank you, Mr. Marks, Miss Macayo," Tori Ann gives us the biggest smile. "For turning this program into something fun and more us."

"Yeah," Scott is actually solemn, raising his cup. "To Mr. and Miss M's!" The other kids join in.

"Cheers," Ryan clinks his plastic cup to mine.

Kim glides over to us to give us the plates and whispers, "You guys are going to make great parents." Ryan and I stand there speechless, letting her comment sink in.

"I don't like this serious crap. Let's keep this party going!" Scott breaks the seriousness, and he highjacks the speakers with his phone. A popular song goes on, and the students sing along and dance.

I stare at the plate given to me, 'The Mom of the Most Amazing Wellington Family Ever' award. I sigh. I haven't had a chance to truly think about Kim and Bryce's offer. I look over to Ryan, who is as deep in thought as I was a moment ago. I gently place my hand on one of his glorious biceps, and he reacts automatically by patting it with his free hand. His eyes are still glazed with many thoughts. "Hey," I gently try to get his attention. He comes back to this moment and smiles down at me. There is an emotion in his eyes that I can't quite comprehend, but it makes me feel good. "Would it be okay if I go? I -"

He nods his head. "No need to explain. Go, I've got them, and I'll lock up too."

"Thank you again for being here, right now." He simply smiles then turns to the kids and begins to laugh, dance, and sing with them. I briefly watch him and the students interact with my own big smile. My heart swells with joy.

• • •

Once I get home, I change into an oversized shirt and take a quick cat nap.

Thirty minutes later, I wake up and prepare a nice hot bath with some scented candles for additional comfort. However, as the water begins to fill the tub, there's a knock at my door. I go to the door and open it slightly with the chain lock still attached. I gasp in shock with Ryan standing on the other side with pizza, two champagne flutes, a bottle of wine, and a bouquet.

"Hey," he says with a smile. "I wanted to celebrate our successful show."

"Um…." I am excited, but then I look down at my minimal amount of clothes. "Would you mind coming back in about thirty minutes?"

"My hands are somewhat full," he presents his bounty to me. "I don't want the pizza to get cold." Sensing my hesitation, he pleads, "Please."

"It's just… I'm not," I stammer.

He gives a gentle smile. "How about this? You let me in, and I'll stay in the kitchen while you do what you need to do."

I sway on the balls of my feet. He's just here as a colleague and neighbor, I remind myself. Plus, keeping him out in the hallway with his hands full is awfully rude.

I gulp, "Okay, hold on." I close the door briefly, unlatching the chain. After I leave the door ajar, allowing him to enter, I hightail it to my room, closing the door behind me. I hear him entering quickly and setting the food down.

"You know, you don't need to dress up on my account," he says loudly.

"What makes you say that?" I try to find a dress from the closet.

"Because the water is still running in the tub."

Oh, shoot! Not thinking about my state of limited dress, I open the door to go to the bathroom, only to find Ryan there, already shutting off the tap. I turn around to go back to my room when he gently takes my elbow. "You look fine. No need to change."

I see both of us breathing heavily as he slowly looks me up and down. "In fact, you are incredibly sexy." I suck air in, not wanting to exhale. He steps right in front of me.

"I thought you said you were staying in the kitchen," I whisper.

"I didn't want flooding in both of our places. That would be too much damage to deal with."

He gently moves a strand of hair behind my ear, before brushing my face. I am shaking. "I don't think I'm in an appropriate attire for a colleague's visit."

His face is right above my head as he murmurs, "How about for your partner?"

He lifts my face and meets my eyes. "If you don't want to do this," he whispers as his face inches closer. "I'll leave you alone." We are nose to nose now. "I promise." I feel the heat of his breath; our eyes search each other to ensure this is what the other person wants.

I finally close my eyes, reach around his neck, and close the gap between our lips. But unlike the kiss we showed the students a few weeks ago, this one passionately increases with each passing second. Somehow he carries me to my room, and I help him shed his shirt. Our kisses grow more fervent, and our hands explore each other's torsos. The back of my knees bumps into the side of my mattress, and we fall together.

His hand finds my shirt's hem, slowly bringing it up. Suddenly I become self-conscious. "Ryan?" I whispered fearfully onto his lips.

My dream man pulls back slightly. I adjust to a sitting position on the bed, pulling my knees up and my shirt down to cover me. He compassionately looks at me. "Isa," he says softly, brushing his thumb on my cheek. "If you're uncomfortable…"

I shake my head. Ryan politely moves over to give me a little more space,

"It's not that I'm uncomfortable… or not entirely at least. I just…" I close my eyes, "I just…" He gently covers my trembling hands with his and gives them a slight squeeze. "I just don't want you to be disappointed," the remaining words tumble out of my mouth in rapid succession.

Silence envelopes the room. Here I am with the guy of my teenage fantasies and my current infatuation. The man I finally begin to entrust myself with. A colleague who works so well with my vision. My neighbor who is willing to give me a hand if I ask. This is Ryan Marks. I am with Ryan Marks. And I stop what is a special connection because my mind and heart are pulsating with fears of rejection. And this particular rejection is something I don't think I'll ever recover from because of how much I have built this up over the years.

A knuckle brushes away a tear that has fallen. "Isa," he says quietly. "Can you please open your eyes and look at me?" Shaking with fear, I acquiesce. His eyes immediately meet mine. Instead of finding frustration, I feel calm with his tenderness. "Why would you think I could ever be disappointed in you?"

I huff. "I'm not as beautiful as your model girlfriend Zoey…" My eyes widen in revelation. Oh my God, I've allowed him to cheat… with me! I have turned him into an adulterer!

"Hang on. You are definitely one of the most brilliant women I have ever met." I open my mouth to argue, but he continues. "And that's both inside and out. You are extremely beautiful, Isa, and I'm not saying that to get into your bed, seeing as I'm already here." He smiles, encouraging me to do the same. "And I haven't had a girlfriend for a while. Zoey was never, is never nor will never be someone I am interested in," he sighs. "I'll be honest getting the attention from a younger woman is thrilling, but she is absolutely daft. I attended a few functions with her to be nice, but that was always the extent of it. I could never return her kisses let alone shag." He brushes my cheek with his thumb. "I don't want a trophy partner, and I certainly don't want to be an object to be used. I want someone with whom I can converse, empathize with, and just connect on multiple levels.

"I feel like in these past months, that's what I get with you. Especially these long hours working together; I never wanted to leave and still wanted to spend more time with you. I'm very much drawn to you, Isa." He gives me one of his easy-going smiles. I melt. He brushes my hair with his fingers, eyes still on mine. "We don't even have to do anything tonight except eat pizza and drink some wine." He stands up and turns to leave.

"I never said I wanted to stop completely…" I whisper; my heart pounding. He turns to me, and his easy-going smile is mixed with a sultry animalistic essence that reaches his eyes.

CHAPTER 20

Sleeping in on a Sunday after the final show is one of my favorite long-standing high school theater traditions. The show is over; no more stressing out about if the mics will work properly, so-and-so will get their lines down, etc. Now it's just time to relax.

I stretch, but my toes touch something that I'm not familiar with. I look around. It is my bed, my room… Suddenly an arm reaches around me. Did last night really happen? I thought I fell asleep when I bathed and somehow managed to go…

"Good morning, love." I freeze. I know this voice. The arm pulls me back to a warm body…oh my.

"Isa?" He kisses the back of my shoulder. "Are you okay, baby?"

This is real. This isn't a dream, and it's not a fantasy. Ryan Marks is really in my bed.

"Would it be wrong if I asked us to stay in bed all day?" I ask incredulously.

"Well, I suppose we could," he responds. I smile, sighing heavily.

Unfortunately, we ultimately decide that we need to be productive, and to do so, we choose not to distract ourselves from each other. Before returning downstairs, I request he leaves me his shirt to keep.

"Come here." He pulls me off the bed and seductively dresses me in his shirt.

I moan. "Keep that up, I won't let you go back downstairs."

"Is that a promise?" he growls.

He finally finishes after a short time (too quickly). He steps back to look at me, "You look better in it than I do." He pulls me to him for some kisses, and with those words, he leaves.

His shirt smells like him.

My cell rings. Oh goodness, it's Sunday dinner time. The best way to ruin my bliss - my sister and mom.

• • •

"I need to make the plans for Thanksgiving and Christmas." My sister is saying this during our weekly video chat.

"Okay…"

"So you will need to be here for both."

"Okay…"

"We go to midnight mass," my mom states.

"Um… it'll be kind of late for me to go back here," I say.

"You stay here. You still have room here."

"I get that… but I really prefer…"

"You stay here. I old, spend time before I die."

There goes the guilt trip thing again; she knows full well that she is healthy. There's a knock at my door.

"I got to go; someone is at the door."

"No, no, no, you stay here."

I groan but keep the chat on. I jump to open the door.

"Hey, beautiful," Ryan, fresh out of the shower, wearing a tight-fitting t-shirt, jeans, and glasses is standing at my door again. "We still have some pizza from last night." He puts his hand on his neck. "I haven't had a chance to go to the store for essentials."

"Luisa!" my mother is shouting on the video conference. "Who is that?"

"Come in. Can't waste a good pizza but shhh…" I whisper opening the door more. He enters and kisses me on the cheek, and he heads to the kitchen and preheats the oven.

"Luisa!" She is relentless.

I return to my chair and face my family.

"You have a boy in your apartment," Angela accuses. Ryan hears and looks around the corner raising his eyebrows.

"Luisa, I want to meet this boy," my mom demands. Ryan motions that he'll do so, but I shake my head.

"Don't shake head at me. I want to meet the boy."

"First of all, unless a boy or girl is related to me…"

"Girl? You and Mia gay?" my mom insinuates. Ryan's eyes go wide.

Angela chortles, "That would make a lot of sense."

"No, Mia and I are not gay. I love her like a sister."

"You don't need another sister. Angela is perfect sister."

"I said like a sister. Angela is obviously my only sibling."

"Ano[11]?" My mom asks to repeat what I just stated.

"She's my only sister," I sigh. "Mia is my best friend…. and there is no boy in my apartment." I peer at Ryan with his mesmerizing eyes and so sexy easy-going smile. I can't help but smile. "I do have a man here."

"Luisa, sino siya[12]?" Again, the question is to request to meet Ryan.

"It's a meeting for school."

Ryan enters the living room, eating a warmed-up slice of pizza. He whispers, "Is that what we did?" He grins.

"Turn video around to see boy."

Ryan comes over to me with a slice of pizza on a small plate. My eyes go wide. "Relax, breathe," he whispers. He brushes off the crumbs his shirt, hands me the plate, and sits with me on the chair. Part of me is on his lap, as the chair is good for only one person. He holds onto me tightly.

"Good afternoon, Mrs. Macayo. Angela, it's good to see you again."

Angela narrows her eyes. "Ryan Marks."

"In the flesh, well, here in Isa's apartment."

"You ambassador's son?" My mom asks.

---

[11] Filipino translation: what

[12] Filipino translation: who is that?

In a tongue-in-cheek manner, Ryan responds. "I am, ma'am."

"Angela says you are…"

"He's here," I interrupt so they do not pry into his private life. "Because he and I are responsible for the winter showcase and spring musical, and we have much planning to do."

"You bring him for Thanksgiving."

"He may…"

Now Ryan interrupts me. "I'd be honored to."

"Good."

"If you'll excuse us, we do have quite a bit to discuss. I look forward to meeting you, Mrs. Macayo. Angela." He pushes the end call button.

CHAPTER 21

I stare at him wide-eyed, not entirely sure what just occurred. It takes me a few moments to realize that Ryan agreed to come home with me for Thanksgiving in a few weeks.

He pulls me completely onto his lap. "Are you all right, baby?" He murmurs on my neck, and I moan at the feeling of his breath on my skin.

I adjust myself to read his eyes, which continue to have a hint of passion. I am at a loss for words, not knowing what to address first. Why is he up here again? What are we doing? Why did he agree to have Thanksgiving with my family?

A look of concern passes on his face, and he squeezes me closer to him. "Baby, what's on your mind?" I open my mouth but close it immediately. He caresses my arm. We sit like that for a few minutes while I try to evaluate my thoughts.

"Are you regretting…" I begin.

He shakes his head immediately. "I don't regret anything, Isa." His sexy, easy-going smile appears. "Quite the contrary, I am relishing all that has happened between us." He leans over to brush my lips with his. "Do you regret it?"

That is the most false statement of the century. I am tempted to tell him that I've been dreaming of this day for decades, but since he doesn't remember me from our student days, I'm afraid saying that will have him running to the hills. In fact, I'm wondering how it is possible that he's still here. I mean, don't get me wrong, I'm really grateful that he's here with me, not Zoey, but I'm also waiting for him to realize that there are better options for him.

In response, I shake my head because I'm over the moon.

"But?" Ryan looks at me, seeing the concern in my eyes. "Are you worried about our ability to not conduct ourselves in a professional manner at work? Because I've been dealing with that for months now," he smirks.

Once again, I can only shake my head because I know my desires have been infiltrating my thoughts during school hours as well.

Instead of talking more, he pulls me closer, allowing me to rest my head on his shoulder and caressing my arm and my thigh. I sigh, capturing this moment in memory. I sneak a peek at his face. His smile is thoughtful and relaxed, and his eyes are closed.

After a moment, my phone rings again. Dang it, I look over, and the ID displays, Mia.

"You're not going to answer it?" he asks after the third ring. I don't because I want to tell her this weekend's events, including Ryan's agreement to attend Thanksgiving with me. Suddenly, I had an idea.

I slowly get up, which elicits a groan from Ryan. "Let's go." I pull him up.

"Where?" he asks.

"Mia and Wesley's."

"Baby…" he stops me and looks me up and down with a smirk. "You really do look amazing in my shirt…"

• • •

After I take a quick shower and don more appropriate clothes, we finally get on the road for our short drive to Mia and Wesley's. We begin talking about everything and anything that comes to mind as there is no possibility of getting distracted completely with each other. Especially me, since I was driving.

"Are you going to clue me in on why we are going to your best friend's house?" he asks.

I shake my head. It seems like I've become mute since the video conference.

"Isa…" he puts his hand on his neck. "I trust you, but I would like to know if you're kidnapping me."

"I promise I'll explain everything when we get there,"

He sighs. "Okay…" An Ed Sheeran song pops up on the radio. "So you like pop music?"

I shrug. "I like a lot of stuff. I'm pretty eclectic when it comes to music." He looks at me sideways. "It really isn't limited to musicals. I promise." There's a brief beat before he smirks. I flip on the turn signal. "Okay, Mr. Marks, since I never get to hear your playlist, what can I expect from it?"

"A little of this, a little of that," he grins. "Maybe a little bit of my band." I raise my eyebrows, glancing at him briefly. "Well, we're on break obviously since I'm here and my bandmates are back home."

"Well, I'm glad you didn't officially break up, and there's still a chance for a reunion."

He chuckles. "Yes, unless you decide to be the Yoko Ono of our group." He reaches out and squeezes my thigh.

I put my hand on my chest. "Lil' ol' me?" I ask with a faux Southern accent, as I park my car in the driveway.

After unfastening his seatbelt, he turns to me, unfastens mine, and pulls me to him. "Don't you play innocent with me? I remember a few times last night that you and I were anything but." His kiss demonstrates his words.

• • •

I open the door. Baskin struggles to meet me at the foyer. It breaks my heart so I leave Ryan to close the door and rush over to the dog for some puppy love. "You're such a good boy!" Ryan approaches, and Baskin begins to growl a bit. I try to calm the dog down. Ryan crouches a couple of feet away and raises his hand to allow the pup to smell his hand. After a few sniffs, the elderly dog calms down, allowing Ryan to pet him.

"This beautiful creature is Baskin," I introduce.

"Hey, boy," Ryan scratches his ears, and the dog sighs.

"It looks like you have another admirer," A voice says above us. Both Ryan and I stand up, and Mia is standing by the kitchen with a twinkle in her eyes. "So you have time to drive here but not enough time to text or pick up the phone?"

"It's post-show Sunday. You know how it goes," I shrug and hug her. She pulls away from me and studies me carefully. One eyebrow rises before a smile appears on her face. She looks to Ryan amused, "What did you do to my best friend?"

I glare at her in complete shock. I haven't said a word about anything. How did she know? Then again she's my best friend.

"Maybe I should've asked first?" Ryan smirks. I catch his eyes, which gleam with playfulness and seduction. My face heats up.

"Do I hear another red-blooded male in the house?" Wesley enters from the family room and offers Ryan his hand. "Welcome, Ryan. Good to see you, man! Want a beer?" Without waiting for a response, Wesley goes to the refrigerator, grabs two cans, and tosses one to Ryan, who catches it easily.

"Thanks, mate," Ryan uses the tab.

"Here for the game? It's not my favorite team, but it is a good rivalry, the Chiefs and the Broncos. Come, take a load off." Wesley gestures for us to follow him, and Ryan begins to go.

"We'll be there in a moment," Mia asks. "I need to have a little talk with this one first."

"Don't be too long," Wesley says. "I'm still not sure how Russell Wilson will be for Denver."

Ryan winks at me with his sexy, easy-going smile before going into the other room with Wesley.

Mia leans over the breakfast counter and simply stares. I know what she wants me to say or confirm, even though Ryan pretty much said as much, so I do my best to hold back and stare back at her.

"You're so sleeping with him now, aren't you?" she hisses happily. Honestly, she would've let fireworks go off if it were available. I bite my lip, neither confirming nor denying.

She gives me a devious smile. "So…"

"Come on, I'm not going to give you details!" I whisper. My face is red.

"Gimme something…" she whines.

"You have Wesley," I say as a matter of fact.

"Yes, I do," she grins. "But freshman Mia remembers all of those nights when her roommate Isa kept babbling on and on about a certain upperclassman."

I sigh and smile at her. She shakes her head. "Nope, I need a little more than that," Mia insists.

I narrow my eyes but giggle. I keep my voice down so the guys in the other room don't hear. "If I say that freshman Isa would die happy, would that be sufficient?"

My best friend balks. "Nope," she grins.

I roll my eyes. "Well, too bad, that's all I'm willing to say."

"You are such a prude!"

"Apparently not…" I give a knowing smile. Mia bursts out laughing.

Without providing any intimate details of our evening and early morning activities, I distract her with the details from the video chat with my family and Ryan. "What am I going to do?"

"He made the decision to go," Mia reminds me.

"Oh gosh," I close my eyes. "They're going to turn him against me. I don't even know what he and I have right now, but once my mom and Angela get their claws on him, he'll leave and never look back."

"You are so overdramatic!" Mia says.

"Can you help me prepare him for this assault that he's going to face?"

"Will it make you feel better?"

Before I can respond, Wesley calls out from the family room. "Babe! Iz! Where are you guys? It's a close game right now! And can you bring us another beer each?"

• • •

After the game, Mia spends a half hour giving a very heated commentary on my family's dysfunctional relationship with me. Ryan takes it all in and asks appropriate questions. We soon take off since it is a school night, but I still have my reservations about him coming along.

"How many beers did you have?" I ask Ryan as we got in the car.

"About five or six," he responds with a laugh. "But that was your plan, wasn't it? To get me drunk, then have your way with me when we get home?"

"No," I state carefully. "That's called sexual assault. I think both you and I would agree that is quite inappropriate and never consider it as foreplay or confuse it with passion."

He nods his head. "You're quite right, milady." He takes my hand and kisses it. "Your friends are great. I miss having my lads around."

"I can imagine. If it wasn't for Mia, I don't know how I'd survived Wellington or even come back here years ago."

He looks at me. His eyes are droopy. Neither of us has had much sleep over the last few months, and I think the alcohol, as minimum as it is, is affecting that.

"Isa," he says softly, kissing my hand again.

"Ryan?"

"Remember those certificates the kids passed around yesterday?"

"Of course, the paper plate awards."

"Yeah… I felt so honored that they would think I would be a good father figure."

"Oh?"

"My dad's a tosser. He hooked up with mum, though he was… is married. I'm shocked he's even on the birth certificate. Never around, that knob. Sent me out here so I won't be ruining his perfect family image." I stay silent but squeeze his hand. "Only good thing he's done is give me money to stay away. The only reason why I've survived being in a mediocre band for years."

I stay quiet for a bit. "So that's why you came back?"

"Andreas emailed me about the choir director position sometime in the spring. I wanted a real way to make a name for myself. I had only taken the money because I resented him." He shakes his head. "So just like he sent me away to preserve whatever he brand he wants to show off, I took this chance to get away from him and his ways to disparage me."

"And how is your mom then?"

"Surviving. I mean, I always make sure that some of the money he throws at me goes to her. I would never want her to suffer because of his inadequacy to truly provide for those lives he has interfered with. I talk to her frequently," he says with his trademark easy-going smile. "She knows that I've been keeping an eye on a certain beauty I work with."

I shake my head. "You are incorrigible."

Ryan looks forward but still holds onto my hand. "When Kim Jensen gave us that creative award, I felt something that I haven't in a long time. Validation, I guess. I don't want to be like my wanker of a dad. I want to be a better man for my wife, my kids…"

"So you're not opposed to having kids, good to know," I don't mean to say that aloud. It is meant for my ever-growing information file. I think his sexy smile appears, but since I want to distract from my word vomit, I ramble. "From the look of our students, you're doing a great job of being better than your dad already. From my perspective, I don't think you'll end up like your dad at all. You make each of the kids feel special; you tell them you're proud of them. You encourage them to be better."

He smiles at me. "My methods mirror a great teacher's I know, so it's only because of her that I'm feeling successful."

I turn to the parking lot behind our building. "Isa, how about you? I mean, do you want a family? Children? I saw you with the two young ones after the first show but knowing about your family dynamics…"

He's a witness to my brief moment of joy with some of my actual family members. "They are Angela's youngest two, Charlotte and Archie. I love them so much." My thoughts return to my office about six weeks ago when Kim and Bryce asked if I would consider adopting their baby girl. I haven't had the opportunity to consider their offer seriously; the timing for their request was just not the best. (Heck, I think Kim even said something to that effect).

Sadly I probably won't even have much time to ponder it until Thanksgiving… in between trying to deal with my family.

    I turn off the engine. "I mean, yes, of course, I want a family of my own…" I hesitate. There is a "but" waiting to be explained. Even though we have this great weekend together, I'm worried that this is as far as it will go. That he deserves and belongs with someone more put together than me. He will find truer happiness with someone other than myself because I will never be good enough for him. That I will just hold him back and how I'm destined to be a spinster.

    We go into the building in silence. As we arrive on the second-floor landing, he pulls me near. "You know our students can be quite intuitive. You are going to be a great mom." He kisses me on the forehead. "Till tomorrow, my dear Isa." He goes into his apartment.

CHAPTER 22

The good news is that Ryan and I didn't completely come unprepared about what is about to happen after the weekend. We know what to do and how to behave, especially since we have to co-direct the next two shows.

That being said, Ryan's description of the student's intuition is as accurate as Mia's day-after observation. The teenagers just know. The kids' knowing smiles and smirks during my classes are almost adorable. Almost.

Ryan comes to my office during lunch and sits on the loveseat while I stay at my desk. We use this time actually to talk about the upcoming showcase. The alumni association set up the theme as "Winter Wonderland" (seriously, these people are supposed to be highly educated with lots of money and winter wonderland is all they can come up with?!), so the acts we choose as entertainment needs to be incorporated within that theme parameter.

"Winter Wonderland?" Ryan muses. "That can go so many directions. Did they just want me to go over the Christmas songs?"

"I don't even know what to do with mini-scenes! Do I do selections from *Frozen*? *Anastasia*? *Frosty the Snowman*?" I shake my head.

He looks at me strangely at my last suggestion. "Are you talking about the claymation TV show?"

I shrug. "Yeah."

"How about *Love Actually,* then?" He suggests.

"That's my favorite Christmas film," I sigh heavily. He chuckles; his eyes twinkle as they read into mine. "I mean, it brings the rom-com aspect to Christmas films without being overly cheesy."

"I can think of a few scenes that will be more appropriate for us to recreate than the students," he winks and heads to my side of the desk. I smirk. "Stacy and Watson have nothing on us, love." He leans over to kiss me.

"Stacy? Watson?"

"Joanna Page… *Gavin and Stacy*. That BBC show James Corden was in…"

I shake my head. "I'm sorry."

"Don't be… I'll catch you up on BBC classics soon."

If my family doesn't scare you off during Thanksgiving break.

"And Watson?"

He brushes a strand of hair out of my face. "Dr. John Watson from *Sherlock*."

I pause for a moment before it clicks in my head. "Bilbo Baggins!" He laughs. I'm grateful that my nerdiness doesn't bother him.

I sit thoughtfully for a moment before slowly envisioning the performances. "I can see *Love Actually* as our motif, especially since it's closer to Valentine's Day than Christmas. Plus, it brings in your quirky Britishness with our unbearable Americanism."

"Well, now that you put it that way." He grins as he reaches for my snack drawer and takes out a bag of chips.

"So that's why you have come here for lunch. To steal my crisps!"

"Now who's sounding more Brit!"

"Well, someone's rubbing off on me…"

He raises one eyebrow. My eyes widen once I realize what I had said. He leans over and whispers seductively, "Maybe later… not maybe, definitely, for sure later." He leans back and grins. The heat off my face is undeniable.

I attempt to bring us back to the topic we initially met about. "Audition day, Monday?"

" I can go with that, but will that be enough time to get to meet up with groups and figure out what act they would like to do? I know I would prefer working with all the singing individuals, duos and groups."

"We can do that once we pick out our cast, but I see your point. How about next Wednesday then? That gives them ample time to decide how they are doing this."

"And we can work on the timeline during fall break while discussing the spring musical."

I sigh. "A lot to do."

"It's a good thing I like spending time with you."

CHAPTER 23

One would think the Winter Showcase is one of the easiest performances to stage since it's basically a student talent show, and the kids have a lot of say about what they want to perform. However, an open talent show that will be performed in front of alumni and local dignitaries brings out all the students whether they are truly interested in performing or not. Ryan's and my job is to weed out iffy content and pull together a coherent show using what they provide us. It's not easy.

Thankfully the students who chose to participate are pretty good. Once we released the parameters of "Love Actually," many acts decide that love songs and dramatic scenes are more than appropriate to be included. Ryan and I evaluate each performance, glancing at each other a couple of times, and speaking through facial expressions. About halfway through the auditions, the dance teacher finally makes his appearance. Sitting on the other side of me, he asks, "So what did I miss?"

"Well, we have several love songs, though if I hear another Taylor Swift song I might just go crazy. Love the girl, but no one can match her." I respond.

"I could've worked with her," Ryan nudges me with a grin.

Christian looks around me and checks out the choir teacher next to me. "I don't think we've met," he flirts. "Christian Denaught, dance."

Ryan offers his hand, which Christian almost topples over me to shake. "Ryan Marks, choir."

I adjust my glasses and hold back a giggle. I don't know whether to be amused or jealous or annoyed that Christian is not only late to the audition but is flirting with my boyfriend. Wait; is Ryan my boyfriend? I give Ryan a sideways glance, and he puts his arm around the back of my seat, his hand massaging my neck. My face goes red. Christian sits back down with a smirk. "So um… you two, huh?"

Gulping, I try to refocus the three of us. "We need to get back on task."

"Um hmmm… lucky bitch," he mumbles.

I look at the dance instructor, agape. "Excuse me! Language!" I try to play it off as if what he called me doesn't offend me.

Christian rolls his eyes, "Puh-lease, Luisa. Like you are this perfect little virgin."

Ryan makes a face suggesting otherwise. Now I turn to him. "How is it that I'm getting attacked by both of you?! Can we please grow up and focus on casting this showcase?"

We finally get through the remainder of the auditions, and Ryan stands and stretches after the final one. Both

Christian and I appreciate his backside. "Damn, what a waste of man…"

"Really, Christian?!"

The dance teacher whispers, "If you get tired of him, you know where to send him."

I take a deep breath. "Seriously, I am not having this conversation with you."

Ryan finally sits back down, "What conversation?"

Christian looks to see how I am going to respond. "Making Scott Webber our emcee. We can have him present each act with different scenes from the film, like Andrew Lincoln's confession posters, the opening airport scene, the prime minister's dance scene…"

"That sounds like a great idea," the choir teacher says, but I see a hint of hesitation.

"We'll write up the script that he has to follow. He'll be happy to have the most important role."

CHAPTER 24

Sadly fall break comes too quickly. I spend the first three days putting together a script so Scott can begin memorizing it once he returns from break. Ryan does assist with describing the film scenes in a way we can use them within the show and which acts will be introduced when. Not saying it is all work, we squeezed in some video games and movies.

Thursday morning arrives, and my nerves force me to wake up. I roll over; Ryan is already wide awake, resting on his elbow with a smile on his face.

"Good morning, sunshine. Happy Thanksgiving," he kisses me lightly.

"Happy Thanksgiving," I mumble back.

He brushes my hair out of my face. "What's wrong, baby?"

"We don't have to go my mom's… or at least you don't."

Ryan smiles gently. "And why not? Are you embarrassed by me?"

I shake my head before laying back down on the pillow. "Of course not."

"Then what is it?"

I give him a frown. "You know she's not my biggest…. fan and my sister…"

"Type A personality," he recalls.

"That's an understatement." He laughs. "Seriously, she's… well, if you do choose to go," I speak slowly. "You'll see."

He leans closer to me. "If you want me there, I'll be happy to go. But I want to do what makes you happy." I sigh heavily. "I can also be there as a support system since it's been suggested that they aren't your biggest supporters. Which I don't understand because I personally think they have a beautiful." He kisses me on my shoulder. "Intelligent." I receive a kiss on my nape. "Creative." Another kiss near my ear. "Talented." On the cheek this time. "Caring." On the nose. "Daughter and sister who is incredibly sexy." The last words tumble out of his mouth in rapid succession. I open my mouth to argue, but he claims that with his own.

After a few moments of kissing, I pull back. "You can't just say stuff like that and kiss me!"

He lies back on his bed with his arms behind his head, grinning. "Well, I can't have you thinking lies are truths either." He turns his head to me. "Honestly, Isa, you are completely incredible."

"I think you're delusional," I quip.

"Nah… just honest."

• • •

We decide to prepare in our individual apartments to save us some time. Before heading upstairs, I told him not to worry about dressing formally, and my family's

Thanksgiving dinners are typically casual. During my not-distracted time, I lay out a more casual dress, not for my family but for Ryan.

He knocks on my door, and his face lights up as I open the entry. "I'm glad I chose this particular jumper," he says kissing me on the cheek. "Now I can look worthy of entering the house with you."

I argue, "You look handsome all time." I close my door and walk out to the parking lot with him.

He opens the passenger door for me, "While I appreciate the compliment, I think it's safe to say that we're trying to make an impression. Meeting the family is a nerve-wracking situation."

I sit quietly as he poises to drive. Meeting the family. Sounds like a relationship type of event. Did we ever define what is happening to us? I mean I should be fine with whatever, but I feel like I need to protect him from my crazy family especially if he's my boyfriend. Don't get me wrong, I will protect him no matter what, but there's something about defining us that makes it concrete.

"Hey, baby," he snaps me out of my thoughts. "Did you put the address on the nav system?"

I go through the touch screen and pull up my childhood home's information. "You know I could just give you directions myself."

He reaches for my hand and kisses it. "Nope. I enjoy these moments with you. Two hours of just getting to know one another more and maybe some Carpool Karaoke?"

A sideways glance shows he is truly ready to just talk, no holds bar, chatting, laughing. And just be us.

• • •

The good times come to an end when we get to the house. There is an unfamiliar car parked in front.

I sit frozen in the passenger side of his car. Ryan once again holds my hand. "Isa?"

"Do we have to go in?"

"Well, we made this long drive…" He reasons before kissing my hand.

I focus on his eyes, "Promise me that we'll leave if I ask."

"Of course," his hazel eyes are filled with concern. I take one more deep breath and open the door. "Hey!" He rushes out to meet me. "I take pleasure in being here for you." He offers his hand to assist in my exit. Not letting go, he uses the fob to lock his car. He rearranges our hands so they are intertwined at the fingers, and we walk into my family home.

• • •

We enter the foyer and little Charlotte runs over to me, yelling,

"Tita Isa!"

Grinning, I crouch down to hug her, but not releasing Ryan's hand. Then she sees someone next to me. She thinks she's whispering in my ear. "Who is he?"

"This is my friend, Mr. Ryan," I explain. "And this Charlotte, one of Angela's twins."

He crouches as well to meet her level and gives her his free hand to shake. Charlotte eyes his hand wearily. "Mommy says not to talk to strangers."

"Okay, then, how about we shake this way?" Ryan releases my hand and flaps his hands, arms, and entire body in the oddest way possible. My niece giggles. "You're silly!"

A deep voice comes from the end of the hall, "Charlotte! What did we say about stranger danger?" The little girl frowns and runs to her father, who is in full dress uniform.

Both Ryan and I rise. "Peter," I motion toward the new figure in the hallway. "Ryan, this is Angela's husband, Pe-"

"Doctor," he insists.

I sigh. "Dr. Peter Pinter."

"Ryan Marks. A pleasure to meet you," Ryan offers his hand, which my brother-in-law looks at with disdain but shakes briefly.

As if on cue, Angela stands next to her husband. Dressed in a cocktail gown, she looks at Ryan. "He is back," she says with a roll of her eyes.

"Nice to see you, too, Angela," my colleague says with a confused smile. He glances at me. I'm unaware of what caused the animosity in her voice.

She looks at his sweater and winces before she takes my outfit in. "Did you get my texts?" She asks sweetly. I shake my head. "We're doing a formal family portrait to send as a Christmas card…. And you're wearing that?!"

"I didn't know about it," I say quietly.

"Well, good thing I had the presence of mind to pick out one of your older dresses. It's on your bed upstairs. We're taking pictures in ten, so shoo." She waves her hand to encourage me to move upstairs. She and Peter then saunter off with little Charlotte in tow.

"I think you look perfect," Ryan says, rubbing my arm.

I try to give him a small smile, but by the reaction on his face, I didn't do a very good job at it. I'm a freaking actress, and I can't even convince my fellow teacher, a fellow actor, that everything is going okay. Maybe I've been wrong all my life. Maybe my mom and my sister are correct. "Um…. I need to change. You can wait in the hallway or um…"

He frowns. "I can wait down here," he mutters.

"I'm sorry," I mumble and run up the stairs. I want to cry. He looks so disappointed, and I just left him downstairs without knowing anyone in this house. I'm a horrible person. The dress lying on my bed… this has got to be a joke… is the dress I wore to prom my sophomore year,

Ryan's senior prom. I close my eyes. I need to get this done… I need to get back to Ryan.

I put it on; it fits like a glove still. He didn't remember me then, so I guess there's no harm.

I put my hair down and touch up my makeup a bit before heading back down the stairs. Ryan wasn't in the foyer, and I don't blame him. I wouldn't want to wait for someone like me either.

I walk to the formal living room. Someone moved the couch so my mom can sit there, and we can surround her.

"Luisa!" My mom cries out, entering the room. She looks me up and down and nods silently. "Angela picks out a good dress for you."

I grit, "Of course, she did." Our mother sits down with an air of royalty. Angela's perfect little family joins. Katie sits to the right of my mother while Charlotte and Archie both take a spot on either side of them. Peter holds Angela in his arms behind the couch. The perfect family.

"Isa! Hurry up or dinner is going to be cold." Angela hisses at me. I sigh and approach the back of the couch. I pose myself and stare out of the hallway in front where Angela's photographer is awaiting to take the picture. Ricky and David look at us approvingly. Then dark hair appears behind the other men, and Ryan looks in. My heart jumps; he is still here. He takes me in, my hair down, my dress. His expression doesn't give away anything, but his eyes…his beautiful hazel eyes show something I can't seem to decipher.

The photographer is easing us up for a picture. "Okay, you all look great. Red," I guess that's me. "Turn a little more towards Angela. Thanks… Okay, ready…"

"Hang on!" Ryan says. Everyone except Angela and Peter is trying to determine who this is. He goes over to me and puts a stray hair behind my ear. I shiver. "Okay, a vision of perfection."

He returns to the doorway, where David begins talking to him. My smile is probably one of the most genuine ones I've ever produced for a family picture. Ryan catches me looking at him and gives me his easy-going smile in return.

Since Angela purposefully scheduled the photography session after I get there, dinner didn't start on time. I introduce Ryan to the rest of the family, without labels, but sadly the only person that seems to treat him (and me) well is David, my cousin's boyfriend.

"Luisa," my mother starts as soon as we all sit at the dinner table. "I wish you come here sooner. Food wouldn't be so cold."

"I wasn't aware that we would have pictures taken today," I mumble.

"We all need to thank Angela for setting up this gathering for us," Peter instructs us with delight. She gives a pageant-style smile, which disappears when she sees

Ryan. "I am so proud to call you my life partner," Peter continues.

"Yes… we have the perfect family!"

Like last time, I pick at my food, keeping my head down. Ryan looks at me with reservation. He slowly attempts to reach out for my hand but quickly decides not to. I sigh.

Ricky then clinks on the glassware with his knife. "I… we," he looks at David. "Have an announcement to make. I said yes!" My entire family squeals.

Little Archie comes up to me and pulls on my dress. "Tita Isa?"

I try to put on a positive face for him. "What's up, sweetheart?"

"What did Tito[13] Ricky say yes to?" Everyone is so focused on that couple that I had a moment to think about it.

"Well, little man, they are going to get married," Ryan answers for me.

---

[13] Filipino translation: Uncle

CHAPTER 25

The first half-hour trip back home is strained. This Thanksgiving is definitely one for the books. Both of us are lost in silent thoughts, but I'm pretty sure we are pondering two different things. After the pictures were taken, I realized that Ryan never touched me again for the day. Sure, he is still the perfect gentleman, by opening doors and ensuring I don't fall and slip on the ice. But there is no more physical contact.

"Thank you," I say softly, watching the scenery change as we drive.

"Thank you for letting me escort you," he replies. His demeanor is still stiff.

"You didn't have to, you know."

"I chose to."

After a few moments, we both speak at the same time.

"Ry-" I start.

"Listen -" He begins. He smirks and waves his hand. "You know the rules, ladies first."

"I need to apologize for my family's behavior."

He holds his hand up. "Stop right there… Never, ever apologize for what your family does. It took me years to learn that." He gives me a quick glance. "They're grown adults; they should know how to conduct themselves."

"I still…"

"I know, I do that all the time too." I look back out the window. "It is an eventful day."

"Yeah," I respond. "I guess it was."

"Not typical at your family dinners?"

"My youngest cousin usually doesn't announce he's getting married to his fiancée so, no I will say not the regular occurrence at family functions."

He drove silently, pensive. "Your niece and nephew are sweet."

I agree. "Yep, they're good kids. Katie is too, but Angela…" I shrug. "Thank you for being so patient with them."

"I really like kids," he says softly.

"Do you have any of your own?"

His one eyebrow rises."None of my own...yet."

I gulp. "I meant to say, nieces and nephews."

He chuckles. "Well, Mum never married, and it was just me and her, as you know. I have a couple of half-siblings, who are both parents I believe. My step-mum never includes me in the family Christmas cards nor even sends me one."

"It's not as virtuous as you think it's meant to be," I state. "Those cards are meant as bragging rights within communities."

"So you won't make one of your own?"

"There's nothing to brag about."

"I beg to differ," he smiles slyly. "You directed a great night of one acts, are doing an amazing job rebuilding the theater program and if I may say so, are quite a vision, which is a very rare thing to find."

"I highly doubt the last one," I snort.

"You're right, I don't want to share you with anyone else." He grins.

"Pretty presumptuous that I would want anyone else," I mumble. Not that anyone wants me.

"Honestly, after seeing your family, I just realize that every family is dysfunctional in their own way. I kind of like that. That I'm not the only cock up in the world." He laughs. "Kind of makes me scared for our kids though…"

I blink a couple of times. Did he say OUR kids?

"Especially with the way the world is headed." Oh, he's talking about the future in general.

"Well, all we can do is raise them the best we can and provide them with every opportunity possible. Limiting their options, their mind, beliefs…those are the things that cause issue and strife ."

"Do you believe in…" In God? Magic? Fate? "Traditions?"

"Traditions," I repeat slowly. "I guess it depends. If the tradition causes bonding and creates a positive lasting comfort, then great. The progressive in me thinks I'm absolutely crazy as traditions can be broken in the interest of the common good. The romantic in me sort of wants how things were done in the past, as long as there is no discrimination."

He nods. "I can see what you're saying…"

Silence falls in the car again. I watch him drive. "Penny for your thoughts."

"Just making a vow to create a more normal real family life than anything you or I ever had…"

CHAPTER 26

The small window between fall and winter break makes me nervous. With the first semester coming to a close, Christian, Ryan, and I all agree that we should minimize rehearsals to have the students focus on their midterms and any final projects they may have to complete. We did remind our cast that we will have full rehearsals upon returning from winter break and remind them to practice with their fellow partners over the break.

Finals week arrives, and on Sunday morning, I prepare my exams. I'm doing my best to keep it analog, so that answers may not be online. That's what I enjoy about theater, we don't always need technology. Euripides, Molière, Shakespeare… they all wrote works that still hold value today, without the requirements of technological advancements. So I am a true believer in using traditional paper for exams and assignments.

A knock on my door gives me a slight break, and Ryan is standing on the other side of the door. With a large grin, I let him in, and he plants a warm kiss on my lips.

"I thought you and I agreed to stay at our own places this week?" I smirk.

"Am I interrupting a date or something?" He asks, looking around. I giggle.

I shake my head. "Just finalizing the exams for the week; I could use a good distraction." I nudge him. "Are you ready for yours?"

"I suppose I am. I mean, a touch of music theory, which the kids are bored out of their minds on, sight reading, and harmonization. I'm sure I can do more, but I don't want to overwhelm myself." He chuckles.

"So it sounds like the perfect idea." I grin.

His hand goes behind his neck. "Actually I do have a question to ask you."

"Did you want something to drink? Snack?" I ask. I'm not avoiding him asking the question; I'm just trying to be a good hostess.

"I'm all right." He reaches for my hand to keep me in place. Oh…what's he doing? Is he going to propose? That's silly, Isa, I reprimand myself. He might be breaking up with me… even though there's nothing to break up from. We never defined what we are. Is he moving and wanting my help? That seems more likely. "I need to know something." I hold my breath. "Isa, do you have a passport?"

A passport? Why in the world would I need a passport? Oh… is he taking me on a romantic vacation? Once again, since we don't have a label for what we are, why would he do something like that?

"Isa? Baby?" He searches my eyes. "Did you hear me?"

"Passport?" I restate his request. I shake my head. "No, unfortunately, I do not. At least not a valid one."

"Oh," he frowns before sitting at the edge of one of the stools.

"May I ask why?"

"Well, I was thinking you could go home with me."

"I do that a lot already," I tease.

"You know what I mean," he says seriously. "I was hoping you would go to the UK and meet Mum. I've already met your family…"

"Wait. I didn't ask you to meet my family." That sounds quite harsh, and he looks taken aback, even giving us more physical space. I suddenly feel awful. "I'm extremely grateful you were there with me that day, but you were the one who agreed to go and I kept trying to give you an out for that day."

"But I went, didn't I? I wanted to prove that this is more than just bloody shagging on my part."

"Okay, and I truly appreciate that we're not just screwing around because I'm vested in it as well, you know." I sigh. "What are we, Ryan? What are we doing?"

He massages his neck again. "I want to say that we are dating, but we have never been on a date, have we?"

I shake my head. "We always seem to forget that part."

"We could try if you'd like. When I get back."

"Get back?"

"I already had a ticket to head back to the UK for Christmas." I simply nod. "I'll return shortly before the beginning of the second term. We can plan on something then." I gulp, thinking of whom he may meet during his time away. I attempt to shake that thought away. He's a grown man, we're not in a serious relationship or whatever, so if he finds someone, it means it wasn't meant to be, right? Or it could just be me.

He tips my chin up. "We'll do something amazing. I promise." He kisses my nose. "Happy Christmas, Isa." He pulls out a necklace from his pocket. I gasp. A charm of the Thalia and Melpomene masks is hanging in the middle. "I hope this is okay until we're back together again."

• • •

The last day before winter break is upon us, and of course, my last class of the semester is my upperclassmen Advanced Acting class. They completed their monologues and written exams with plenty of time before they are released for break. The class is spending time within their groups. Bryce is giving Kim a massage, while she chats with her roommate Tori Ann and Willa. Jordy and some other boys goof off and almost break a lighting kit, which provokes Kacey. In a surprising turn of events, Scott is the only one who is doing any type of theater-based activity, memorizing the emcee script.

"Miss Macayo," Tori Ann interrupts my blissful dreamlike state as I oversee the rest of the class. "Are you excited?"

"Excited for what?"

The girls giggle. Bryce rolls his eyes but provides a big smile. "For your trip to London of course!"

"Excuse me?"

"With Mr. Marks?" Willa adds. "Isn't that his Christmas present for you?"

My hand automatically fingers the necklace that is on my neck. "No…"

"Strange because he's been kinda in this trance. He seems really excited about it."

"Well, I wish he or you guys would have actually given me a heads up, but mine is expired."

"Who doesn't have a passport?" Jordy snorts. A crumbled-up piece of paper is thrown at his head.

"My dad has some contacts at the State Department," Kim offers.

"I'm sure he does, and then what? As far as I know, his flight leaves today."

Scott finally breaks character. "Wait… isn't that the opening of this Love Actually movie? Or a big part of it? You could do what that little kid did and sneak pass security to tell him how you love him."

"Wait, what?!" I stare at my class, chuckling. "First of all, I am not as flexible or as fast as Ferb is in the movie."

Several of the kids ponder my statement. "Ferb? Like 'Phineas and Ferb'?"

I smile. "You guys didn't know that little Sam and Joanna from this film are the voice actors for Ferb and

Vanessa?" The kids noisily discuss their favorite cartoons growing up, distracting them from asking more personal questions.

However, one group doesn't take the bait.

"You love him, don't you, Miss Macayo?" Kim grins.

In an attempt to create another distraction, I play confused. "Ferb?"

"Mister Marks," Willa giggles. The class quiets down a bit more, waiting for my response.

"Wow…" I pause, not sure what to say. I mean, I've had this crush on Ryan for years. Do I truly love him? "Guys and gals, this isn't a rom-com movie."

Bryce smirks, "That kiss says otherwise." Jordy wiggles his eyebrows.

"A kiss that was nearly two months ago?"

"And that's why he always asks about you in class?" Kacey provides.

"You all are dreaming." I smile.

"Oh come on," Scott says. "As the emcee for the Showcase," the kids groan at this statement. "I get the privilege of also being the Christmas angel that gets to tell you what you're really feeling and what you're not seeing."

The class erupts and argues about Scott's supposed position. I can't help but laugh. These kids are a silver lining to my otherwise dreary start to winter break.

• • •

The faculty lounge hosts our post-exam gathering, but I opt to go home. Ryan should be boarding his flight now; he had been to the airport soon after the end of the first class of the day, which is the only one with an exam.

Despite the cooler weather, I decide to walk today. All the pent-up energy from finals, Ryan, and everything in between needs a way to get out, so walking it is. The plan is to allow myself to clear my mind before heading to my mom's house for the ever-so-exciting Christmas that my lovely sister has planned. Two wonderful days of reminders of how I'm not living to their standards. At least I get to spend the week after with me, myself, and I until New Years' Eve when I get to spend it with Mia, Wesley, and some of their friends. Wow, I need to get a life.

Reminder: Ryan comes back shortly after New Year, so I just need to last until then. But with no communication with him during this time (I made it clear that it would best if he should spend all the time with his family and friends there and not texting, chatting or video conferencing me), it's going to be quite a challenge.

• • •

I receive a text from Wesley in the midmorning of December 24. I don't think much of it as I am being forced to stay the night at my childhood home tonight and I focus on preparing. About five minutes later, another text just before it becomes a continuous stream. I curiously pick up the phone to read the text. He's asking me to come over as soon as possible, even going as far as making sure he's wearing clothes this time. (Something I never ever thought I had to confirm before going to my best friend's house). I reply that I'm just finishing up my packing and heading out in the next five minutes.

Once I get to Wesley's and Mia's house, I don't bother rushing in, so knock on the door. I don't want to ring the doorbell and encourage Baskin to bark like crazy. (Although I think a knock would have triggered yelping too). Wes answers. His eyes are red, and his demeanor is solemn. My stomach drops. Something truly feels off. My face probably pales as every worst scenario about Mia fills my head. "Thanks for coming, Iz. She's in the family room."

I run through the house to find her sitting on the floor with Baskin in her arms. She is sobbing. I rush over to her, "Mia! What's wrong?" I give her the biggest hug I can.

"We have to let him go…" She cries loudly. Baskin attempts to look up, but he is struggling to even breathe.

Tears well up in my eyes. I turned to Wesley, who is standing near the kitchen; his own face wet from tears. I allow my tears to flow freely and begin stroking Baskin's head. I attempt to calm my voice to a steady cadence. "You're a good boy, Baskin. You are such a good boy."

Wesley gives each of us a bottle of water and motions me to go to the kitchen. I know he's going to tell me everything as we both know that Mia is inconsolable and won't be talking much.

"We realized it last week," he begins. "Baskin just wasn't eating any of his food and simply lying there. I took him to the vet, and they said there's not much we can do. He's just out of time. I didn't want to do this right before Christmas, so I avoided telling Mia." I know that it's eating him alive that he couldn't tell her. They tell each other everything, no secrets between them. "But this morning, we had a difficult time waking him up. He just couldn't anymore. I've let him suffer longer to keep Mia happy. Thankfully the vet can come here and give him his final moments at home."

I nod, my own tears not slowing down either. "I know that she'll be better with you around, too," he continues. "And knowing your family history…"

"I'm staying here. You guys are my family too."

The doorbell rings. Mia sobs louder. Wes and I glance at each other sadly before I attempt to be an anchor to my best friend in this difficult time.

• • •

After the final goodbyes to Baskin, Wesley and I do everything we can to calm Mia down. We force her to eat pizza, since no one cooked for Christmas Eve, and drink water, to keep her from getting dehydrated. Wesley finally drives to the nearest pharmacy to get one of those nonhabit-forming sleeping pills. I do whatever I can to keep her distracted.

"I can't believe he's gone," she whines. I'm pretty sure she was bone dry from crying too much.

"But he's in a better place," I reassure her. "Remember all dogs go to heaven.."

"That's a cartoon, Isa!" I can tell she wants to shed more tears if she isn't dry already.

"And who says it isn't true? Can't you picture it, getting to heaven and God letting all the puppies loose on us?" I attempt a small smile.

"But I want him here now! He was a good dog!" She puts her head down on the bar.

I don't know what to say, so I just rub her back. Thankfully, Wesley returns and takes over.

By the time, she falls asleep with her boyfriend next to her, it is 9:30 pm. There is no way I'm driving to my mom's house, so I drive home before calling them.

CHAPTER 27

"Where are you?" Angela scolds me over the phone. No video conferencing, just good old-fashioned voice transmission.

I sigh. My eyes and cheeks are raw from all the tears I experienced earlier. I do not want to deal with this. "There was an emergency, and it is too late to drive out there."

"What could be more important than us?" Plenty…. The family I've formed with the people here who actually care about me.

"I'm emotionally drained, I'm exhausted. A two-hour drive would not be wise," I argue with reason.

"Are you only staying out there because of Ryan Marks?" The snide doesn't go unnoticed. I roll my eyes.

"He's in the UK," I state coolly.

She laughs evilly. "Probably mooching off his ambassador sperm daddy."

"He's visiting his mom," I say flatly.

"Whatever… you need to be here tomorrow." She hangs up. I groan, not wanting to think about what twisted story she'll be telling our mom about my absence.

• • •

I begrudgingly start the long drive early Christmas morning. I make a quick stop at Wesley and Mia's, but once I arrive in the driveway, I couldn't bring myself to get out of the car and open the door, knowing that grief is waiting on the other side. I simply pull out and head to the interstate.

Christmas music is blasting on all over the air radio stations, as it has been over the last couple of months. Since it's Christmas, and I require show tunes, I connect my Bluetooth and put on the soundtrack to the first act of *RENT*, which of course screams Christmas as much as *It's A Wonderful Life*, *A Christmas Carol*, and *Holiday Inn*. (Although I guess *Elf* and *A Christmas Story* can be added to the list as it has grown in popularity on stage).

The music provide some ease during the two-hour travel time, in which I sang along with the music for the entirety of the ride. However, upon my arrival, I cannot help but sigh as to what is waiting for me inside my childhood home. I take the kids' presents out of the trunk and head inside.

The smell of Filipino food automatically brings a smile to my face. The aroma of pancit[14], calderetta[15], and adobo fills the air, and for once, I'm not cringing as much as I usually do when I have to participate in family activities.

As always, the twins are the first to rush to me. They hug my legs, and I put my packages down before scooping them up for a big group hug.

---

[14] A Filipino noodle dish

[15] A Filipino beef stew

"Santa came! Santa came!" Charlotte is bouncing off the walls.

"Is this for us?" Archie greedily gazes at the things I put down.

"Maybe," I reply. "I'm so happy that you guys are happy." I squeeze them again.

A snort forces me to look up. Their father is standing in the hallway. "No boy toy for you this time?"

"Merry Christmas to you too, Peter," I respond as the twins run back to the family room, where I know the Christmas tree and the majority of the presents are always located. I pick up the gifts and head back to where the kids ran off to.

"What kind of a person leaves their sister to take care of their family celebrations instead of choosing to spend time with some fling?"

I pause when he says that word. Fling?

"Ryan is in the UK visiting his mom. I had to deal with a crisis."

"You're just a school teacher," my brother-in-law scoffs. "What kind of a crisis do you have during a vacation period?"

My temperature rises with my anger. They are so flippant about my job. I want to respond with an attitude back, but to prevent drama, I walk away.

"Luisa!" My mother shrills as I put the kids' gifts under the tree.

"Maligayang Pasko[16], po[17], Nanay," I smile at my matriarch as I wish her a Merry Christmas. However, the scowl on her face, makes my forced happiness disappear. Here we go.

"Why did you not come here last night?"

I sighed. "I had to deal with a crisis."

"I thought it's vacation." She glares at me. "No school. Is it that boy you bring with you on Thanksgiving?"

"No." My response is quiet but strong. "Mia and Wesley had a problem."

Of course, Angela enters the room at that exact moment. "Did she finally reveal to him that she's in love with you?" She smirks.

"You two gay?" My mother asks.

"No!" I sigh and look around to make sure none of the kids are around. "They had to put their dog down yesterday."

"On Christmas Eve?" Angela snorts. "Please you can make up a better excuse than that. Plus no one would put a dog above family. That's just stupid."

"A pet is family," I point out.

"Whatever."

---

[16] Filipino translation: Merry Christmas

[17] Filipino translation: An added supplement to show respect for one's elders or commanding officers.

"You miss mass because of a dog?" My mom clarifies. I blankly nod. "Selfish girl. Family is more important. Your Ate wouldn't do that."

Did she just call me selfish? Because I put my family circle above my biological family? I feel my face turning red. The anger continues to rise with each person I encounter in this house.

Angela loudly requests for her children and husband to go into the room. As she distributes the gifts, I notice that Katie's pile gets taller than either of the twins; she's receiving about twice as much. I raise my eyebrows. Once the wrapping paper is cleared off, I notice that the value for each item is greater in value for the oldest child. I get chills about the nepotism playing out in the next generation.

"Ka ka ina[18]," Nanay announces it is time to eat. The twins come up to each family member to thank them and wish them a Merry Christmas; their older sister, however, rolls her eyes and plays on her phone.

I walk into the kitchen to drink a large cup of water. I don't want to blow my top, but it's getting to be very obvious what Angela is doing. My sister and husband walk into the room. "Are you going to help us out or be a useless brat today?" Peter laughs, taking the rice to the dining room. Angela laughs along with him.

---

[18] Filipino translation: Let's eat

I shake my head at my sister. "You will never change, will you?"

She sneers at me. "What are you talking about?'

"You know exactly what I mean. You are turning Katie into a mini you, complete with the narcissistic nature."

She grins. "There is absolutely nothing wrong with Katie. She already looks like me and has my brain. The twins," she winces. "They're more like…. Well, not me."

"Are you really that self-centered?"

"Are you really that much of a drama queen?" She laughs. "Or is this stemming from the fact that you are not as good as me?"

I shake my head and hiss. "You are flippin' out of your mind!"

"Oh, poor Isa, Mom and Dad don't pay as much attention to you. Never mind the fact that they celebrate my achievements and me all the time because I earn them. I became a doctor. You squandered… yourself; you'll never live up to your potential. No one wants you." She sneers. "Don't you ever tell me, a pediatrician, how to raise my kids because you will never have your own family."

She and I stare at each other. I want to slap her so badly. She rolls her eyes. "You are so worthless." And takes a bowl of pancit with her.

If I am a cartoon character, steam would be coming out of my ears right now. Surprisingly I'm not crying nor backing down, but I need to leave. I cannot be here anymore.

I take the large bowl of the stew and place it down in the center. "I'm very sorry, but I have to leave."

"Seriously," Angela says offhandedly. "You're going to ruin our Christmas because you're butt hurt?"

"No," I stated defiantly. "I'm leaving because I need to."

"Selfish," my mother repeats.

"You can say that. I know words shouldn't hurt me," I stare at my mom and my sister. "And at Christmas, you tell the truth." I quote *Love Actually* then inhale deeply, "I need to surround myself with people who love me and support me for being me. Not who you think I should be, but me. Merry Christmas." I walk out and drive off without looking back. A huge weight lifts off my shoulder.

CHAPTER 28

The week between Christmas and New Year is extremely lonely. Normally I am at Wesley's and Mia's, but I wanted to give them space since the events of Christmas Eve. And the only other person I probably would say something to is on another continent and is radio silent at my behest. But here I am.

Busying myself is not a problem. Without having to worry if I'm bothering my downstairs neighbor, I rearrange my furniture to give it a fresh look. I finalize the lesson plans for the remainder of the year and create new classes that can be taught under the theater banner. I also consider collaborative classes with the choir department and dance, which I have to clear with those specific instructors when we return.

I am just finalizing some of my plans, when I receive a text from Mia, asking to open the door for her. It's the first time I've smiled in days… heck, it's the first time I've had any sort of human interaction.

Sprinting down the stairs, I open the door, and her smile is over the moon. "Bestie!" She pulls me in for a huge hug. After all that happened last week, I'm thrilled she's in a better mood. However, I'm cautiously optimistic if this is genuine joy or if she's just trying to put on a stronger facade to hide her true feelings.

Heading up the stairs, she pauses at the second-floor landing, looking at Ryan's door. "When does your boyfriend get back?"

"He's not…"

"Okay then, when is your colleague who you spend nights with…"

My face is hot and probably red as a clown's nose. I shake my head, "You are hopeless." I head up the next flight of stairs to my apartment. I project the next statement as she is almost at my heel. "He returns the day before the semester starts."

Mia whistles. "Cutting it close, isn't he?"

I shrug, opening my door. "This was scheduled way before the school year even began. Actually, it was part of the terms of his hiring, I think." I drop my keys onto the bowl, but they fell to the ground. I suddenly recall my redecorating spree over my last few lonely days.

"I like what you've done to the place!" She plops herself down onto the couch. "I think this opens this place a lot more."

I go to the kitchen and return with two cups of coffee. Handing one to her, I see her eyes twinkling. She's glowing. I hold back the cup as she reaches for it. "Wait… are you pregnant?!"

"What?" She snaps back at me. "Girl, you're crazy!" She grabs the coffee I initially hand to her. She clasps it with both hands, and my face just bursts into a grin. The sunlight reflects on a diamond ring on her finger!

She and I look at each and scream. "Oh my gosh!" She put her cup down, and we stand up, hugging and jumping in excitement.

After two minutes, we finally collapse back on the couch. She drinks her coffee as I grasp her left hand, admiring her ring. "Twenty years later…." I state it.

She shakes her head. "You and I know that in all technicality since Wes and I have been pretty much married this whole time. I guess we're just making it official now."

"Still wow!" I fall into a giggle fit, and she joins me. "I'm so happy for you!"

"I know you would be."

"How did he propose?"

"Nothing extravagant. Just Christmas morning." She frowns. "I think he still feels bad about Baskin, which I'll admit was…" I don't let her finish that thought and simply pat her hand to let her know I understand. "So I think this might have been a way to distract me from going full-on depression mode."

"Or he could have been planning this for awhile." I rub her arm reassuringly. "As you said, this is just to make it legal."

"Yeah…" She smiles. "So, my maid of honor, you better be free on New Year's Eve…" She raises one eyebrow.

"Of course!"

CHAPTER 29

Thankfully the plan does not include going to Las Vegas because honestly, any huge crowds on New Year's Eve would be a disaster. Same with Time Square. Nope. I would have loved to live in New York but would definitely leave during those super crowded days.

Instead, Wesley and Mia book a few rooms at a hotel in Stonehaven. The property is also holding a countdown party starting at 11:00 for all their guests over the age of 21. I guess that would make a cool reception since Wesley's brother and I are the only two people attending the unification event.

I am tasked to bring Mia to the hotel and prepare her there. Actually, I insist on this. This wedding isn't typical in any way, but I make sure there are some of the traditional nuances on it. I guess it's the hopeless romantic in me.

We enter my room and place her dress in the closet before we crash on the bed. "Do you realize that this is the final time we get to hang out together as single ladies?"

She snorts. "Are you saying we should do the Beyoncé dance?" She and I look at each other and grin. Without another word, I find the song on Spotify, and we are poorly dancing the choreography. We are laughing uncontrollably.,

"We got the last appointment at the salon," she tells me after we order room service. Apparently, they are going all out for tonight.

"Remind me again why at the very last appointment? Isn't that at 9:00 pm?"

"Pretty close," she replies.

"And what time is the wedding?"

"11:50 pm. So our first kiss as husband and wife will be in the new year." She grins. "What a way to kick off the new year?"

I return the enthusiasm on her face.

• • •

The rest of the evening is the first time I was genuinely happy during the winter break. The salon does an amazing job with Mia's updo and makeup, giving me a little more vibrancy in my hair and face. Returning to my room, I assist her with her white tea-length dress with a bright purple sash, which fits her perfectly.

I look at her up and down with approval. "Okay, checklist!"

"Seriously, Iz…"

"Something new?" I ask anyways.

"The dress, of course."

"Something old?"

"My panties," she guffaws. I make a face, and she grins even more. "It won't stay on for too long…"

I put my left hand up. "T-M-I right there."

My best friend laughs even more. "I was going to call you prude again, but I know a certain music teacher who would prove that statement incorrect."

I roll my eyes. "Something borrowed. Something blue."

"Your blue topaz earrings." Mia gently flicks them.

"Okay. Lemme text them that we're off to the bridal room next to the roof so neither of you will see each other."

"Really, Iz? Following this is so tedious and lame," the bride complains. The text is out, and I peer around the door before escorting my best friend out of my room before she becomes Mrs. Wesley Devens.

The hotel staff is preparing the main ballroom for the party. The balcony, where the ceremony is to take place, is closed off until after midnight. There is a little room off the side where Mia does all her last-minute preparations. Around 11:15, when I know the bar is functional, I offer to get us something to drink.

The hotel guests are starting to pile in. I already regret the decision to come out here, but I know the bride would like some spirited refreshment. I finally make it to one of the counters and make our order. As I wait for the mixologists to prepare our drinks, I people-watch. It's amusing to see who is around to ring the new year with a bunch of strangers.

"Well, look at you, bouncing back so quickly!" A familiar voice takes me away from my trance. Christian Denaught is looking sharp tonight.

"Hey, you!" I grin at him but am quite perplexed at what he said. Bounce back? How did he know my family drama from Christmas? "Happy New Year!" I offer to give him a half hug, which he accepts right back.

"Happy New Year is right, sister!" His breath smells like the drinking started way before this shindig. "Good way to get rid of all the negativity from this past year."

"That's a good outlook."

"Lemme see." He reaches for my hand and gives me a twirl. My bridesmaid's dress was a simple midnight A-line cocktail party dress. He nods approvingly. "Ryan Marks would be kicking himself for letting you go."

"I'm sorry, what?" The confusion permeates my face, but it seems to not faze him.

"Zoey whatever has nothing on you. She's such a…" he makes a face. "And if Ryan, as hot as he is, can't see that… then he's an idiot." He leans to me, "I've got your back, Luisa." He pulls away. "But right now, I've got my eye on a very good-looking man over there." With that, he walks over to an attractive young man at the other end of the room.

The bartender brings me my two drinks, and I sign the receipt to charge to my room. Maneuvering through the crowd with two drinks held high, Christian's revelations still run through my mind.

I kick the door, so I don't spill the drinks. Mia opens the door and looks at the party. "There are a lot of people out there," she closes the door. I hand her the cocktail. She takes it gratefully and then studies my face as she drinks from the straw. "Are you okay?"

"My best friend is getting married. I'm more than okay!" I force a grin.

"I know you're missing Ryan right now, so we won't force you to stay past the ceremony," she says gently. "Hell, if Wes wasn't here, I'd be out of it too."

"Sweetheart, tonight is about you and Wesley, and I'm more than thrilled to be standing next to you guys on this next chapter in life."

"You make it sound like it's a giant step or something," Mia laughs. "It's just formalities. Everything will be the same."

There is a knock at the fire door, and Wesley's 27-year-old brother, Derek, checks on us. "Ready? The officiant would like to get going."

I check the time on my cell. The new year is happening in 15 minutes, which means the wedding starts in five minutes.

· · ·

The short but sweet ceremony makes me tear up, but to be honest, I don't know if it was because of the wedding, what Christian had said, or seriously being by myself tonight. However, with both a photographer and a videographer capturing this intimate event, I make sure a smile is present on my face and pray it reaches the rest of my body to seem genuine.

Suddenly the crowd inside begins the countdown to midnight. Thankfully the officiant keeps everything timed correctly. "I now pronounce you husband and wife. You may kiss your bride in four… three… two… one…" Wesley pulls Mia in for a kiss, and the fireworks appear in the night sky. After a lot of hugs and the patio door to the main ballroom opening, the new year is in full swing. I look around and see that Christian dancing with the guy he was eyeing. Derek offers to dance with me, but I insist that he can do better. So I direct his gaze to a woman that was watching the ceremony the whole time. Wesley and Mia join in the festivities with most of the crowd offering their congratulations. I stay back to watch the crowd.

I also take the opportunity to look into what Christian said. The first thing I look up is Zoey Waines' social media pages. While I found some tame pictures on Facebook, I notice she reposts a lot of stuff from a Zoey LaAmour's account. Clicking on the link, I find myself on Zoey LaAmour's Instagram page, and the first picture and caption that make my stomach drop.

Zoey shows off a giant diamond ring with Ryan in the background, smiling. The picture's geotag states London. And the caption reads, "I am going to be Mrs. Ryan Marks!"

CHAPTER 30

The toughest part of this new semester is keeping a smile on my face. I'm an actress, darn it. I shouldn't be wearing my emotions on my sleeve. Instead, I create a teacher persona from a nonexistent play to portray. Perhaps it's the only way I can get through this difficult time.

At least Mia and Wesley's elopement truly brings joy to my heart, and I'm so blessed they asked me to be a part of it. Of course, it will take a while to call them husband and wife, but I know this is just a formality since I never doubt that they are meant to be forever.

After my first class, I sit in my office and have lunch. I pick at the salad I made for today, when lo and behold, Ryan appears at the classroom doorway.

"Hey, love," he says, and although he has bags under his eyes, his smile reaches his pupils. I shiver slightly, even though I am heartbroken.

I avoid eye contact and mumble, "Hey!"

He peers at the outside corridor before fully entering my office. He walks toward me but then stops. I guess he sees that I am not interested. "Is everything okay, Isa?"

I force a smile. "Fine."

He shakes his head. "Then it isn't all right," he sits on the loveseat but keeps his eyes on me. "Are the students affecting you too?"

"The kids are great," I shrug. "Why would they affect me?"

"Oh yeah, you don't have the upperclassmen yet," he reaches behind his neck. "You know how you say that something is off?" I stab a piece of lettuce and stare at him without verbal acknowledgment. "Well, it felt like that during my first-period class."

I wanted to ask more, curious about what had happened, and find a way to comfort him. But then I remember that he has his new fiancée, Zoey, to do just that. So I just stuff vegetables in my mouth and chew thoughtfully.

"Could you ask them for me? Please?" he asks me. I shake my head. "Are you miffed, too? Is that why you wouldn't answer the door last night? Or any of my text?"

I glare at him, finally swallowing my salad and my pride. "It doesn't seem like I'm a necessary part of your life, Mr. Marks."

He looks at me very confused. "What do you mean?"

I drop my fork onto my desk and stare at him. "Two weeks ago, you informed me that you wanted to date me, but it seems like a load of crock now in retrospect."

"Is it because I haven't asked you out on an official date? I wanted to do things properly."

"And because I said I couldn't go home with you, you find the next available girl who will swoon all over you to meet your mom and propose?"

"Isa," he stands up and looks me directly in the eye. "I really have no idea what the hell you are talking about."

I rise from my chair, lips tightly sealed. "Everyone in the school knows, Mr. Marks."

"Would you stop calling me that? And I love the fact that the school knows how happy I am."

My heart breaks. Literally stops beating. I am just a toy to him, and this is his little game. I blink away tears and collapse in my chair, my head in my hands, avoiding any eye contact again. "Well, congratulations then," I whisper. "Please close the door on your way out."

I don't know how long before he left, but once the door shut, tears began to flow freely down my face.

• • •

"Are you okay, Miss Macayo?' Tori Ann hugs me upon entering the studio for their Advanced Acting Class. "I can't believe this shit."

"Victoria Ann… " I give her a fair warning about her language.

"Sorry," she mumbles.

After a good five-minute pity-me-cry fest, I ensure I look presentable for this class. I go into full-teacher mode, using that fake play in my head. That teacher, I remind myself, doesn't give a crap about what her colleagues do in their private lives as it doesn't affect her.

"I know full well what is happening, and I can tell you that I am okay with it. I need to focus on the showcase and spring musical."

The teenager nods her head. "Those of us who are in performance choir made sure he knows how we feel about the whole thing."

I raise my eyebrows. "So he spoke to you all about the engagement."

She shakes her head this time. "No, but I wish he did because many of us would have walked out in anger."

"Oh, sweetie," I sigh. "Don't endanger your grades for something that probably wasn't meant to be."

"No offense, Miss Macayo, but are you kidding me?" I tilt my head, waiting for a further explanation. "You two were meant to be together. You're supposed to be. I didn't witness that kiss …" I sigh again. "But everyone who did told everyone else how much they would love to have even a sliver of that love between the two of you."

"I'm sorry to shatter your and everyone else's fantasy, it seems it was all a misunderstanding. We were acting to show…"

She interrupts me. "To show Willa and Jordy how it's done? Do you actually believe that, Miss Macayo? Because we are witnesses to the after-kiss bliss that you and Mr. Marks have."

The other students file into class. My "teacher mode" smiles. "Unfortunately, Tori Ann, love isn't always the answer in life."

CHAPTER 31

The end of Christmas break signals crunch time for the showcase. Once the kids return, they have two full weeks until showtime. I set up the timeline on what performances will be occurring at what time and at which stages. The thought of having a date makes me sick. My typical backup, Mia, is required to work the event as a liaison for the town.

But my love life is not my priority right now. I watch the three freshmen do a song and dance routine that hasn't been honed down yet. They keep running into each other and forgetting which part will be sung by whom. I close my eyes. I understand they had a break, but today's technology does allow them to connect even with the distance.

I look around, waiting for the door to open and for Ryan to come marching in to help fix this. While I do have choir experience, this is his department. The dance teacher, Christian Denaught, is making notes to figure out how to assist the girls, but he can only do so much as well. My co-director is dropping the ball on this one.

Thankfully, my student director, Kim, is on top of it. The problem is she's seven months pregnant and can only handle so much. She looks at me, wincing. "Do you want me to find Mr. Marks? I can text Bryce to find him…"

I shake my head. "It's okay, Kim. I can handle this." She gives me a sideways glance as I stand up, clapping my hands. Thankfully all the students pause to clap and await directions. "Um… can we take five, ladies? I need a quick break… Please talk to Mr. Denaught." The dance teacher narrows his eyes at me, and I shrug. I take my phone and head to my office. I close all the doors and bury my head in the crook of my arm. I am doing the best I can to keep it together. I don't want to ask for help, especially not from him.

• • •

Despite not having Ryan show up at every rehearsal, we manage to pull off a decent show. Both Kim and Bryce step up more than the fall production, as did most of the upperclassmen. Even Scott keeps his ego at bay and becomes more handy in the technical aspect of the show. I'm just praying that this isn't because of Ryan's lack of participation. I don't think it's fair for the kids to have to step up because a teacher isn't holding up his end of the production.

To be fair on the rare occasion that Ryan is at rehearsal, he acts professionally and gives his full attention to what's going on. And the kids have admitted that he does use his regular class hours to work with those who have a musical number in the show. So at least there's that.

As far as my feelings are concerned, well, I miss him. I truly miss him. And not just being physically intimate with him, I miss just talking to him, hanging out with him, and being comfortable with him. It sucks that I can't feel at ease with him because I feel so betrayed.

"Have you even given him the chance to explain what happened?" Mia asks me when I am over at her place the Saturday before the Benefit.

"I don't know if I can accept it. You know pictures are worth a thousand words." I sigh. "I just feel like I've been duped way too many times between my family and him."

"Well, I wouldn't put it passed the floozy to pull some shit of her own either," my best friend reminds me.

"He was in the picture, Mi. It'd be one thing if he wasn't, but he was there, clear as day, smiling and looking at the camera." I shake my head. "He's never denied to me, the students, or other faculty members."

"So who are going with to the Benefit?"

I shrug. "I'll go stag."

"Like hell you are. You are not showing up without someone. It bites that I'm working that night." She sighs. "But you will not give Ryan and Zoey the satisfaction by being there by yourself."

CHAPTER 32

I am grateful that Wesley escorts me to the Benefit. I told him he could at least hang out with his wife, which is still weird for me to say, but I'm so happy for them. With a smile plastered on my face, I mingle with the alumni and the local bigwigs, thanking them for their contribution to the school. Many did stop to let me know that they are super proud of the entertainment and hope that this scholarship allows more local students to attend. I spot Ryan and Zoey talking to his friend Colin and his wife; I swallow the champagne I've been nursing and walk in the other direction.

"Hey, you want to do a platonic slow dance?" Wesley asks me.

I raise my eyebrows and look around him at Mia, who winks at me. "Mia put you up to it?"

He shrugs, fixing his tie. "She told me that you look upset. I don't know. I thought you were smiling."

I really love my best friend right now. "Okay. Only if we make it awkward like a middle school dance with a balloon in between us, leaving room for the Holy Spirit."

My best friend's husband grins. "Deal."

So we keep each other at arm's length as we sway to the music. "So, who do you think AFC champions will be?"

"You want me to say Denver, don't you," Wesley laughs. I attempt to smile but spy Zoey palming Ryan's chest and speaking very close to his face. I scowl. "Okay, I won't say Las Vegas then!" Wesley replies.

I shake my head. "Sorry. I got distracted."

My dance partner glances over in the direction of Ryan and company. "You know he still wants you, right?"

I tsk. "I'm not what he wants. I'm not good enough for him, and he'll regret it if we were to make something more permanent."

Wes looks down at me. "Look, you've been like a little sister to me since Mia and I began dating, and I have treated you as such."

"Yeah?"

"I know Mia is the only one who calls out your bull and doesn't sugarcoat jack. That's why I love her, but since you're her best friend and she's my wife, I want to have a little leeway for what about to say." He pauses; I'm wondering if this is for dramatic effect. "Get your head out of your ass, Isa."

I stand there agape. "You are not bad luck. Not everyone is against you… there may be some people like that pixie stick there and your insane sister who are determined to make your life a living hell, but that means you're doing something right."

My eyebrows rise as I glare at him. I use a moment to take in all he says. "I wasn't saying that I feel bad…"

"Isa," Wesley interrupts, turning us around. "I want you to look over there, and you'll see what I'm talking about."

I slowly peek around my dance partner and meet Ryan's eyes. A part of me wants to turn my head away, but I attempt to read what his eyes are saying. There is something, the same emotion that I often catch when it's just the two of us... At least before winter break. Nowadays, I usually get a blank expression back. I sigh sadly before turning my head away. My heart feels even more broken; I don't know if there's anything I can do to repair it.

•••

Dr. Teague approaches me toward the end of the night. "Luisa, it's typically your job as the theater instructor to give the final thank you's before the final act."

"Yes, sir." The speech is on notecards in my purse.

"Ryan requested if he could make the final speech tonight. I figured you wouldn't mind."

Mind? The guy broke my heart, barely had anything to do with rehearsals, and wants final credit? Yes, I mind! "Of course not, sir."

"Thank you." He winks at me. "You all did a great job putting this together."

"Thank you, sir."

I'll be honest, I am a bit angry. He goes behind my back to pull this?

Ryan gets up on the main stage and clears his throat. "Good evening, everyone." We all pause to look at him. "My name is Ryan Marks, and I am the choir director at

Wellingworth as well as an alumnus. I want to thank you for taking the time on a Saturday evening to help raise funds for our students. I've seen firsthand how your donations and support impact the school and the community. And if you enjoyed tonight's entertainment and wait staff, you also experienced how your money goes to work. Can we please give a round of applause for all the student volunteers for making this happen?" There is clapping all around the room. I will admit I admire how well he's pulling this speech together without notes. Is he doing this off the cuff?

"We do have some more acknowledgments before I give back to our emcee, senior Scott Webber." There are some hooting and hollering from the volunteers, and Scott gives off a goofy grin. "First, thank you to Dr. Andreas Teague, the administrative staff, and the board of directors for always directing the school toward the path our founders intended…" The routine of clapping and Ryan's acknowledgments goes on for about two or three more moments. He breaks the tempo to grab the acoustic guitar at the edge of the stage while mentioning Christian.

The choir director pauses and begins to tune his guitar. He looks around the room until his gaze lands on me, and he begins to strum his guitar. "And finally, a very special thank you to the woman who organized tonight's entertainment, theater director Luisa Macayo."

He begins to sing as he accompanies himself, "It's not you, she says. It's just that life's so hard." The song is from Jonathan Larson's *tick, tick… BOOM!,* "See Her Smile", but it isn't featured in the Netflix film. "We all get blue I say. Hang on tight - I'll be your bodyguard. Something's breaking my baby's heart; something's breaking my Isa's heart, something's breaking my baby's heart… Oh - I just want to see YOU smile."

My heart mends itself more at each mention of my name and the other minor change from her to you. He makes it personal. He's singing it to me, and his eyes stay on mine except for when he makes chord changes. "… I just want to see her… I just want to see you…" He finishes the final chords and sings the last word a cappella while focusing deep into my eyes. "Smile." I blink away happy tears and bite my bottom lip. He returns his sexy easy-going smile at me. The applause is thundering.

"Mr. Webber, I think it's time to wrap this up." Ryan transitions it back to Scott before he puts his guitar back on its stand. I start walking in his direction, but I also notice Zoey storming toward him. He turns around and walks in my direction with a grin. Unfortunately, Zoey reaches him first. Shoot… did I imagine the song is for me? Or was I daydreaming? I change direction and head out to the hallway.

Once out of the room, I pray for understanding for the situation and the patience and knowledge to deal with it peacefully.

The door opens. Ryan stops in front of me; his beautiful hazel eyes are searching mine, his thumb brushing my cheek. "I've missed you."

"I missed you, too." He tilts my chin up and brushes his lips on mine. The door opens again, and that's when chaos ensues.

"You bastard!" Zoey screams at him. She storms up to me and once again tries to slap my face, but this time Ryan is the one to stop her arm. "She's a whore and a home wrecker!"

"Zoey," Ryan's face is beet red; his words are stern and to the point. "I don't know why you feel you have any input here, but I will not allow you to talk to Isa this way."

"I am your fiancée," she roars, still trying to get an audience who would listen.

"What?!" He looks baffled.

"You proposed to me in London."

"I did no such thing."

"I met your mom, and she is excited about our wedding."

He raises an eyebrow, shaking his head in unbelief. He then turns to me. "Is this why you've been upset with me?" I open my mouth to respond, but he glared back at Zoey. "None of those things happened! You are delusional and need to leave us alone. If you continue to spread these vicious falsehoods, I will be forced to file for a restraining order and sue for libel."

She huffs. "You can't do that. I own Waines Hall."

"Your parents donated it to the school. The school owns the building. Not you."

"Zoey," I pipe up gently. "Maybe you need to go home and rest; we can discuss this all Monday morning with Dr. Teague."

"Shut up, you fu-" the 24-year-old starts.

"Dude, she's saving your ass again!" Jordy is behind us with some other students. "Seriously, you are one crazy bitch!"

"Jordan!" I turn to him to warn him about respect.

"So a bunch of gangsters thinks they can threaten me?" Zoey scoffs.

The rage on the kids' faces is rising, and Ryan's expression is equally peeved. I take a deep breath. "Zoey, you have a beef with me, fine, but we need to handle this on Monday or even in private, away from the students and with an unbiased moderator. Please stop embarrassing yourself and the school, who is your employer…"

"I'm a public figure…"

"And strangers are filming your actions now," Bryce retorts. "What kind of publicity would that bring you?"

"Your sponsors will leave your ass," Kacey adds.

"This isn't over," she threatens both Ryan and me. She storms off.

"And take down that stupid ass post!" Kacey yells after her.

"Thank you, guys, but please return to the benefit," I sigh.

It takes a moment, and Ryan places his forehead on mine before the kids finally return to benefit. I sigh deeply. "Why do I feel like I feel like she's not going to let this go?"

He shrugs. "But now we can face it together. Don't ever let her get in between us again, please…" I raise my eyebrows. "And I promise the same thing."

CHAPTER 33

Another Sunday after a show, I sleep in, but only because I made sure Ryan went home at a reasonable hour the night before or early this morning. I remember that we agreed to go on a date before returning to our relational proclivities. I admit though I miss waking up in his arms.

What I do wake up to is pretty impressive for not being physically together.

> good morning sunshine
> i miss you

>> good morning! I wish you are here!

> Me 2

> dinner 2nite?

> pick you up @ 6

>> Can't wait.

>> Dress code?

> Your smile

>> Already wearing it.

> promise me youll wear only that when I make dinner here

> I thought we agreed to have an actual date

> 2nite yes but im thinking for future dates

I roll my eyes but giggle.

> You're incorrigible.

> But

He knows I never end a conversation in this manner, so I begin to type.

> I love you and won't trade you in for the entire world

I reread what I typed and decide it may be too much. After all, I haven't said those three words aloud to him yet, and who knows how he really feels about me. Instead, I reassure him with the latter words only.

> I won't trade you in for the entire world.

6:00 pm cannot come soon enough.

• • •

Although he never officially clarifies the dress code, I choose to wear a simple black dress that is versatile for anywhere, including a fast food joint… Okay, maybe it's overkill for a drive-thru and a movie. But from what Ryan has previously hinted, I think it will be more than that. Maybe. Plus it would be really good to see him in a suit or out of one. I'll have to keep reminding myself to get my mind out of the gutter.

He knocks on the door at 6:00 pm sharp. I open my door, and we look over each other. He's wearing a black button-down with a silver tie and khaki-colored slacks. I lick my lips. He looks great.

"You are a sight for sore eyes." He pulls me in for a kiss. "I don't know if I can keep my hands off you tonight."

"You know I won't be opposed to staying home…"

"But we agreed actually to date and prove this more than casual shag," he sighs. He nips my ear and whispers, "I know we're more than just two people who are good in bed together."

There's a twinkle in his eyes when he meets mine. It is more than passion in it; understanding, caring, and friendship, just to name a few. All qualities that make a solid relationship, despite each other's flaws.

I give him a peck on the lips. "Thank you."

"We better go. We do have a reservation."

Grabbing my midi peacoat, and stopping briefly at his apartment to get a warm coat of his own, we walk to our destination, an upscale Italian restaurant, Floriente. "I had to pull some favors to get us a table tonight," he winks. He opens the door for me, and the atmosphere is truly perfect upon entering. Dean Martin's "On an Evening in Roma" plays on the speakers, and the smell of fresh basil and garlic wafts through the air.

The hostess sits us in an intimate booth and takes our drink orders. The dark corner is lit with a candle and some dim recessed lighting. "I must admit, I'm impressed. You must have bribed the busboy to get us such an amazing table." I attempt to sip some water with a very thin smile, but I don't think it's working.

Ryan laughs heartily. "Shhh… don't tell them the secret; otherwise, we'll never get this table again."

"So I take it he told you about this place." I'm sure we are both talking about Bryce at this point.

"He wouldn't stop telling me to take you here. I think he wants something over the class."

"He's a good kid." Ryan concurs with a nod. "But we shouldn't be discussing the students or the school."

The waiter drops off our drinks and takes meal orders. "I agree. I missed you so much," he kisses my hand. "And when I couldn't comfort you, I was bloody gutted."

"I'm sorry that I jumped to conclusion. I need to work on not being so gullible."

"Guarded is probably a better word." He takes a swig of his beer. "I mean after the negativity your family throws at you, I don't blame you. I know exactly how you feel." His jaw tenses.

"I know," I whisper. "I actually might not be on the best terms with them right now. I haven't heard from them since Christmas." My chin is down; I never realized that it is affecting me emotionally.

He tips my head up. "What happened?"

"I blew up at Angela. It started with how she puts Katie on a pedestal, and the twins get pushed aside." I bite my lip. "And it sort of escalated."

"And you feel guilty?" He puts a strand of hair behind my ear.

I blink a couple of times. Do I? I mean, I miss our chats but do I feel guilty for letting it all out in the open? "Maybe not guilty. Maybe more lonely. With Baskin then Mia and Wesley's wedding…"

His eyes widen. "Wedding?" He massages his neck. "I missed quite a bit." I nod. "Baskin is their dog, correct?"

I look down at my lap again. "Was."

Ryan rubs my arm. "Oh baby,… When was this?"

"He stopped responding to early Christmas Eve, and by midday, the vet came by, and we had to say goodbye." I sniffle

"You were there? Baby…" He pulls me close.

I put my head on his shoulder. The waiter places the delicious plates of food in front of us, but instead of letting go, Ryan continues to hold me.

I swallow and adjust myself. "Enough about my crappy break. How was yours since you clearly didn't get engaged? How is your mom?"

"Mum is doing well. I told her about you, and she says we'd have to video conference sometime." He cuts off a piece of his steak and chews it thoughtfully. After swallowing it, he looks at me. "Isa, we can't do the same thing that we did this Christmas break. You needed someone to talk to; we need to be able to connect." He kisses my free hand before taking another bite of steak.

"Oh, come on," I twirl the pasta into my fork. "I know that Old Joe enjoys midnight chats…" I wink with a grin before taking a bite of my angel hair pasta with Marsala sauce.

"I'm serious, Baby," he says. "You went through a traumatic event, and more and more things keep piling up… and who did you talk to?"

"I'm not completely inept, I can make friends. The baristas, the local parents, including Bryce's mom."

This time he brushes a knuckle on my cheek. "You said you were lonely, I never want you to feel like that again… I lo-"

"Would you some dessert? Coffee?" The waiter interrupts.

"Could you give us a moment, please?" Although the waiter obliged his request, Ryan and I both know the moment has passed. There's no chance I'll hear him say what he was going to say. His hand squeezes my hand. "Hey, I appreciate you were trying to give my mum and lads and me time, but I wanted to see you too. I missed you so much."

I sigh. "You keep saying that. But then again, I feel the same way in a more stalker-type way maybe."

He bursts out laughing. "My girlfriend is a stalker?" My heart is full of joy.

CHAPTER 34

Monday morning rolls by too fast, and before I know it, we are in full drone mode with no breaks until Spring Break around Easter. This also means that there is limited time to choose a musical. We need to get moving, and I email the choir and dance teachers to meet on stage after school.

Christian, Ryan, and I meet on stage. Although I can safely say that ultimately I can call whatever show I want (not one of the five Stein had on continuous rotation for a school), I'm trying to be fair. We each had Bluetooth speakers with our playlists on our phones ready to go, tablets with librettos, and my laptop to make the final purchase.

"Thank you for meeting today," I tell the guys.

"As if it's a stretch for Ryan to spend time with you," Christian says dryly.

"Hey, I'm just here for the snacks," My boyfriend (Pinch me! It's real! No more second guessing) finds one of the cool ranch Doritos bags and takes a dramatic bite of the first chip as he wiggles his eyebrows at me.

"She is going to make you sleep on the couch…" Christian laughs. "Pass me a Frito's please." I throw him a bag. "Much obliged."

"Game Plan…" I start.

"Dwayne 'The Rock' Johnson," Ryan replies.

"Ooooh," Christian smiles slyly. "That is one beautiful man. Is he your celebrity pass?"

"We get celebrity passes?" Ryan's one eyebrow rises.

I shake my head. "Ladies, can we please focus? We don't have much time left."

"We have three months, Love," Ryan argues, pulling me close and kissing my forehead.

"Hello! Desperate single guy here!" Christian waves his hand. "Please control the PDA!"

"Back to planning, I was thinking something more age appropriate and contemporary. While I love the classics, I think we can reel in more interested parties this way."

"So more Pasek & Paul, Miranda, Bareilles and Tracz." The choir director connects with me on so many levels.

"Most of the characters who are less than 5 years older or younger that the kids." Christian reiterates.

"Even though this falls directly within our parameters, can we just say right now, no *High School Musical*?"

"Agreed." The men say in unison.

"Let's just say no Disney in general."

"Yup." I take a grateful breath that they both agree.

"Well, here are some considerations: *West Side Story, Les Miserables, Heathers, Be More Chill, Dear Evan Hansen, Waitress, Hamilton, Into the Woods, Putnam County Spelling Bee, Anastasia, Charlie Brown, Harry Potter*…"

"*Harry Potter* isn't a musical!" Christian snorts.

"Actually Darren Criss and StarKid Productions put one together."

"It's pretty hilarious, mate. Look it up on YouTube."

"Anyhoo… hoo… hoo… Get it?" I receive odd looks from both guys. "Harry Potter? Owl?"

Ryan and Christian groan. "Baby, you are sexy, intelligent, talented, kind…" My face turns red with each compliment. "But comedy is not one of your strongest attributes." He kisses me on the nose.

Christian shakes his head. "Continue to rub my solitary life with this…"

"What happened to the guy from the hotel?" I blurt out.

"Now who's turning this into a sorority meeting?" Ryan murmurs. I stick my tongue out at him, and he shakes his head with a very playful look in his eyes.

"One and done," the dance teacher sighs. "Hard to find a good man around here."

I frown, and Ryan replies. "Sorry, can't help you there, mate." Christian simply shrugs.

"With an exception of Mia and Wes's wedding, New Year's Eve was kind of a letdown," I comment quietly.

"Hey, I didn't mean to cause a strain in your first few weeks of this year," the dance teacher apologizes to us. "She's like Regina George…."

"Who?" Ryan is super confused.

"The reference or what I am alluding to?"

"I know the refer-" he pauses and picks up my laptop.

Christian and I exchange glances this time, "Care to fill us in?"

"The rights have been released," he grins and catches my eyes. "I know what our spring musical is…"

CHAPTER 35

During the third week of rehearsals, I work with Christian to ensure they can start their dance where I have them standing. Kim is sitting in the second row; her swollen feet are elevated on the seat in front of her. Bryce keeps looking at her from the wing, worried. Ryan steps into the auditorium and sits in the back. I guess he already released the group that he's working with for the night.

The kids have been working on the same two pages as it leads straight to the choreography. However, since we're not off-book yet, Christian is frustrated because some actors are still holding on to their scripts.

"Luisa!" The dance teacher grits his teeth at me. "Must we start with the lines or can we simply just do the dance?"

There is a cry in the audience, and Kim is wincing. We all look at her. Bryce walks out of the wing, "Are you okay, Kimmy?"

"I think it's just gas," she says with a smile. Ryan looks at our students with concern and walks to the teen boy. I'm not sure what's transpiring, but I do my best to focus on the scene we are working on.

"Can't you work with my choreography?" Christian haughtily asks.

"Listen, I know that the dancing is important, but we need to get make sure the lines are properly delivered to push the story."

"Everyone knows this story!" Another cry. "We've all watched the film."

I think I hear my name, but I'm not sure so I continue to stand my ground with our choreographer.

"But we have to assume not everyone has."

"Well, it's stupid," Christian continues.

"Isa," There is more urgency in the voice now, but since Christian is ticking me off, I opt to focus on that discussion.

The dance teacher dares to request the next thing. "Can't we just require them to watch it? I mean, it should be streaming on something."

"Are you off your rocker?"

"Miss Macayo!" Ryan's voice booms from the house. I turn to him, wondering if he is going to reprimand me for going off on a fellow teacher, but instead, I see a slight panic in his eyes. "You have to go now."

"Ooooo…." Willa says slyly. "Date night?"

I shake my head, and he nods to Kim, who is wincing again. He holds up seven fingers. It takes me a moment to realize that he is telling me that there are seven minutes between contractions. My eyes go wide.

"You know what, Mr. Denaught? Yeah, just choreo for right now please." I gave him the motion to move the students to either one of our studios to prevent a bigger scene

"Let's work on it in my classroom," he instructs the kids, who move quickly. He glances down at the pregnant teenager. "Good luck." I hurry off the stage.

Ryan leans over to update me. "I have Bryce getting something for me in my room. I can bring him and Tori Ann to the hospital. You have permission to take her alone, right?" I nod. He takes my keys and hands me my tote before brushing his lips softly on my cheek. I sigh but compose myself for Kim's sake. "I'll pull your car around. I'll meet outside you in three."

I look at my student. I can see she is in slight pain, but she just continues to rub her belly. I crouch down next to her. "Hey, Kim, Mr. Marks is getting my car so I can take you to the hospital. He'll take Bryce and Tori Ann there after rehearsal. We need to keep Bryce as calm as possible to keep you calm." She nods and makes a face. "Deep breaths." I help her get up, and as quietly as possible we move up the aisle.

• • •

I manage to get us to the hospital calmly. I was never there for Angela's pregnancies, and with Mia being my best and only real friend, I am never privy to having any of my other acquaintances' and colleagues' private lives. So here I am, playing surrogate mom to one of my students as she delivers a new life into the world.

Upon arriving at the hospital, the staff rolls her to one of the delivery rooms. I inform them that I will only be here for a little while, but after a contraction, Kim asks me to stay. I nod and tell her I will be here until she no longer needs me. Once it is just the two of us, I look at her in awe.

"I can't tell you how proud I am of you. You are so strong, kiddo."

"Thanks, Miss Macayo." She begins to tear up and squeezes my hand. Another contraction. After that subsides, she brings me back to several months ago. "I know we've been busy and whatnot, but Bryce and I would really prefer you to be the mom of our little girl. We want to know that she will grow up with love, affection, and most of all theater." I laugh. "We're serious, Miss Macayo, and I promise that we won't interfere. She'll be your little girl; we're like doting relatives."

"Kim…" The door bursts open, and Bryce comes running in, with Tori Ann right on his trail. Ryan more or less strolls behind the two students.

"They kept me at the school, Kimmy! I'm so sorry!" He kisses her. "I'm not too late, right?"

"She's still pregnant, you putz!" Tori Ann reaches for her friend. "How are you holding up?"

As a response, another contraction forces Kim to squeeze her boyfriend's and her roommate's hands. The other two groan in pain. I shake my hand that Kim had a death grip on earlier; it's not ideal, to say the least.

"Bryce, did you call your mom?" I asked.

"He called on the way over here." Ryan stands next to me, slowly caressing my back. I continue to watch in awe as three of my students look more like adults than many of their peers. Their responsible nature, kindness, and love should be replicated by many in the world today. I'm so proud to be their teacher.

A nurse comes and realizes there are three more people in the room. She looks at us, "So are you two the adoptive parents of the baby?"

"Er…" Ryan's spare hand reaches for his neck.

With a hint of hesitation, I respond quietly, "No." My fellow teacher gives me a sideways glance.

"We are responsible for the three," Ryan adds, nodding to the teenagers.

The nurse tsks. "If you were really responsible, she wouldn't be here in this situation in the first place."

I glare at her. Ryan scoffs, "You have no right to pass judgment on us or them."

The older lady huffs. "Maybe, but you have no right to be in here then. And neither are they." She indicates toward Bryce and Tori Ann. "Her mother just called. She'll be here shortly with the adoptive parents."

"What adoptive parents?" I ask.

"I am not at liberty to tell you that nor even say more to you. Now if you don't want me to call security, you and those teenagers must leave the room. Her mother has medical power of attorney and demands that no one else is in the delivery room except her and she is the sole person to make any decisions."

"It's her body," I state. "She's not keeping the baby, but she has a right to say who can and cannot be in the room!"

"This is a private hospital," the nurse replies tersely. "And I'm not going to tell you again to leave the room."

Ryan places his hand on the small of my back, which is usually my cue to leave. I'm fuming at this point. "Isa," he whispers in my ear. "Let's go… we'll be in the lobby." He leads me out of the room but immediately returns to calmly get the other two teens. Bryce is fighting him, and Kim's screaming and yelling.

Tori Ann meets me in the nearest waiting room. "I'm going to call my dad!" She announces with tears in her eyes. I continue to look at the corridor waiting for Ryan and Bryce.

"Luisa," someone calls out my name. I see Francine Powers, Bryce's mom. She comes and hugs me. "Am I too late?"

I shake my head. "They kicked us out."

"They kicked you out?" She repeats. Ryan slightly pushes Bryce by the shoulder out to the waiting room.

"Mom!" Bryce calls out. "They wouldn't let me stay to make sure she's okay. She's alone in there." He gulps a large amount of air, and tears are ready to fall from his eyes. She reaches out for her much taller son, and he crumbles in her arms and sobs into her shoulder as if he was a toddler again.

Ryan stands next to me; his face is mixed with emotions. "I… er, better go," he whispers to me. "You're much closer to them. I'll update Andreas and see if I can help out with damage control." I nod. "Keep me updated, and I'll do the same." He squeezes both Tori Ann's and Bryce's shoulders. At the door, he does turn to look at me with a small albeit encouraging smile before leaving.

"Augh!" Tori Ann throws her phone onto one of the uncomfortable chairs. "Dad says we can't do anything because this is a private institution. Their policies can be held up." She finally releases her tears. "I thought human rights laws supersede private corporations!" She sobs, and I sit next to her, rubbing her upper back gently.

My phone buzzes, and I look down to see who it is. Ryan is warning us that there is trouble walking in the door. I go to Francine, who is comforting her son the best she can. "The Representative's wife is coming."

I see the fire in her eyes. "Good," Bryce's mother is ready. "There are a few things I need to settle with her."

Joanie Jensen walks in with purpose, avoids any eye contact with us, and heads to her daughter's room. Both Francine and I glare at her.

Francine squares her shoulder. "I need to do this… She can't do this to my child or my grandchild." She murmurs something to Bryce, who is finally calming down, before standing up to confront Kim's mom.

However, a security guard blocks us into the waiting room. "You all need to leave. You are not guests of any patients, and you are not patients yourselves."

I feel tense, and my hand balls up to a fist. "You know this is wrong."

The large security guard flickers a sympathetic look but covers it up quickly with an icy emotionless stare. "Just go."

Francine holds Bryce up, and I encourage Tori Ann to go back to the dorms. We silently go to our separate vehicles with only a nod between us. As I open the driver's door, a new luxury electric car parks next to mine, and a woman around my age emerges. I recognize her but am unsure who she is.

She glances at me with a smile. "I'm having a baby!"

I nod, tired and emotionally drained. "Congratulations."

She beams. "Thank you! Colin and I have been trying for so long!" She gives me a joyous hug before running to the main entrance.

• • •

During my drive back to campus, it dawns on me who she was. She is Ryan's friend's wife.

• • •

I drop off Tori Ann back at the residences fifteen minutes before curfew before proceeding to my apartment building. The trudge up the stairs feels heavy, and Ryan keeps his door wide open as an invitation to visit. I stand still to decide on closing the door gently and heading up the second flight of stairs. Old Joe looks at me curiously as I walk by his place but doesn't say anything. I just nod as I pass him.

CHAPTER 36

As we expect, Bryce and Kim are absent from class the next day. Tori Ann is forcing herself to attend classes, but one can see in her eyes, she is not concentrating. During my third block Advanced Acting class, there is a melancholy air in the room, especially as most of these students are either in the cast and/or friends of the young couple.

I'll admit I wasn't up to teaching either. In fact, because of my emotional and physical state, I decide to allow all my classes to watch the teen film our production is based on. But to make it a more educational distraction, the classes have to compare and contrast the two mediums (film and stage) in which the story is presented. And I emphasize to them (well, mainly Scott who would have a silly comment about everything) that stage production having a song and dance component while the film is mostly void of that is not a valid argument.

Dr. Teague summons me to a meeting after school. I text Ryan to be in charge of rehearsals until I can get there but am informed that he is busy as well. Sighing, I ask Christian before leaving the building. The dance teacher surprisingly acquiesces without much prodding, even confirming which scenes the kids are to be working on.

In the main office lobby, I sit in the less comfortable chairs, adjusting how I am seated a few times. Jane

Tromberg stares at me for a bit; I cannot read the expression on her face. The door opens, and Dr. Teague gestures me into his office.

As I enter, I see someone sitting on the group of chairs, but since it was facing the other way, I am still determining who it is. I await for direction from my boss, who is still at the entrance as if he is waiting for someone, who appears within moments. Ryan. His hazel eyes meet mine. Without a word, we both know our curiosity is at the forefront of each other's minds.

Dr. Teague gravely gives us instructions to sit. I approach the circle of chairs and find Joanie Jensen occupying one chair. I sit opposite her, and Ryan takes the chair next to me. The headmaster continues to stand to take the rein in this meeting. "Mrs. Jensen brought up a couple of things that she wants to address about your involvement with her daughter's…" he pauses. "Predicament."

I look over at Ryan. He flattens his hand, palm down, telling me to stay calm. I then turn to Kim's mother.

"It has come to my attention that the two of you are involved in attempting to keep Kimberly hostage in this school."

What?! "Come again."

"She lied about coming home last summer and during all holiday breaks, and you two are to blame for her delinquency."

"Excuse me," I say. "How is this our fault? Mr. Marks arrived here at the very beginning of the fall semester, and I did not see Kim until move-in day." Ryan quickly reaches out and squeezes my hand to defuse my rising temper.

"You have an obligation to inform the parents what is happening with their children," the representative's wife menacingly informs us.

"If they are doing something illegal or dangerous that can cause harm or cost them their lives," I counter.

"Well, then Bryce Billings kidnapped her, endangering her, and you are in concert with his actions. I will be filing a police report to indict him of the crime and you as an accomplice." She says this directly to me.

Dr. Teague holds his hand up. "Mrs. Jensen, there's no need for that."

"Then I want her fired for insubordination!"

"She has done nothing that warrants dismissal," Ryan pipes up in my defense.

"I beg to differ," Joanie Jensen scoffs. "She transported my daughter alone in her vehicle without my or the Representative's consent."

"You signed off a blanket permission slip allowing us, staff and faculty members, to drive them to medical appointments or emergencies," I respond. "All families of those residing on campus during the school year does so." Ryan squeezes my hand again.

Mrs. Jensen huffs. She doesn't like how this is going. "Then I want Bryce Billings expelled for kidnapping!"

I feel my hand turn into a fist under Ryan's palm. He attempts to calm me down, but I feel him shaking with anger as well.

"It is my understanding that your daughter consented to be with Mr. Billings and his mother for the duration of the breaks," Ryan explains. "It seems as if they are keeping her safe from those who mean to do her harm or neglect." There is a veil of an accusatory tone in his voice. "I'm sure Miss Macayo and Dr. Teague, as well as your own child, will agree with my assessment."

She glares at him. "I'm sure if the Representative speaks to your father, Mr. Marks, the Ambassador will see things our way."

This time it was my turn to squeeze Ryan's hand and continue holding it tightly. Dr. Teague speaks tersely, "There is no need to bring anyone else into this situation, Mrs. Jensen. I'm sure we can come up with a compromise that will work for all of us."

"Pull Bryce Billing's scholarship effectively immediately." I gasp. This woman is vindictive. "I don't want my Kimberly to see him anymore."

"He has less than two years left here!" I argue. "Why are you trying to ruin his life?!"

"He," she starts with disdain in her voice. "Ruined my daughter's life."

"How?" I ask. "By being in love with her? By taking care of her? Kim and Bryce approached me months ago about adopting the baby." Ryan looks at me shocked at the revelation. "They explained to me how they came to this decision. They acknowledged and assessed their situation and made a decision that is best for both the child and themselves. Their maturity level is far more superior than all of us in the room combined."

Ryan's hand pulls away from mine. Suddenly I feel cold and alone in this fight.

"Mrs. Jensen," Dr. Teague calmly speaks up. "I'd like to inform you that Kimberly's grades did not falter at all during her… situation. In fact, I seem to see a slight improvement."

Joanie Jensen is fuming. "If you do not revoke his scholarship, I will pull Kimberly out of this horrible institution."

I groan. "Are you serious? She too is just shy of a couple of years from graduation! I know that's not what she wants. And I know that you would not want the stigma of the inquiry on why Kim isn't graduating from here."

"Are you threatening me?" She accuses me. "You do know who I am right?"

Ryan finally speaks up. "If Dr. Teague agrees to pull Mr. Billing's scholarship, will you allow Kimberly to finish school here and not accuse Mr. Billing, his mother, Miss

Macayo, Wellingworth, or I of any wrongdoing against your family?"

Dr. Teague and I glare at him. His face is stone-cold at this point. The Representative's wife takes her time to respond. "Yes."

Ryan looks at Dr. Teague. "Can we have Miss Tromberg put this agreement in writing and all parties sign in agreement?"

"Mr. Marks…" the headmaster begins; however, something I am not privy to makes our boss agree to the terms Ryan has lain on the table. "Miss Macayo, please inform Miss Tromberg to come in here, and you are free to return to rehearsals as I'm sure the students need their director." There is a finality in his tone, saying I am not to stick around after this. I nod and try to catch Ryan's eyes, but my fellow instructor avoids me. I do what I was asked.

• • •

Just like the rest of the day, the auditorium has an air of hopelessness. I thank Christian for going over the scene and allowing the students to keep the blocking suggested to them by the choreographer. However, the lines feel flat with zero emotions. I run through the scenes quickly and end rehearsals early.

• • •

I drive home as quickly as possible, hoping to catch Ryan before he turns in for the night. His car is already parked when I get there. So I hurry up the stairs and knock on his door several times. "Ryan, it's me," I say with a few knocks. "Please open the door." However, after a few minutes, I still don't get a response from him.

Old Joe, however, steps out of his place. He instructs sternly, "Luisa, go up to your apartment."

"But…" I begin to argue.

"Trust him." He points to Ryan's door. "Trust me. And most important of all, trust Him," he points to heaven. Trust God.

I gulp down the tears and nod, trudging up the stairs. There's no one I can talk to about this because the only other person I can discuss this with refuses to give me any more time.

CHAPTER 37

As expected, the school returns to normal… well, newer normal beginning the following week after Kim's delivery. From what I hear both Kim and Bryce are back on campus, and the two of them are still inseparable. I can't confirm, though, as their theater class is tomorrow.

Since I didn't hear from Ryan all weekend, I decide to go to his office for lunch, and I brought some Cool Ranch Doritos as a peace offering. I wait until his final second period class exits the main classroom, where many smile and greet me.

I head inside and meekly knock on the office door. Ryan raises his head from the sheet music he's evaluating. His lips stay thin, but if I'm reading his eyes correctly, he's glad I stop by. "Miss Macayo," he stands and looks around the corner, "I've dismissed all the students, correct?"

"I believe so, I saw plenty of them when I came in."

He closes the door. His happiness is finally reflected in his smile and pulls me in for a kiss. "Been too long," he murmurs when we finally pull apart.

I hold up the Doritos. "So you don't want this then?" He tries to grab it, but I put it behind my back. He smirks and wraps his arms around me again with another kiss, and I easily release the bag into his hands. After the kiss though, he holds me tight before parting again. "You are too good to me, but I still missed you this weekend." He kisses me on the forehead and plops himself onto one of the guest chairs in his office.

"I wasn't the one avoiding you." I sit down on the other chair.

He pulls the chair closer to himself and puts his forehead on mine. "I'm very sorry about that. I needed to do this myself, and make sure you have zero culpability if she reneges."

"What's going on? Why did you allow her to take away Bryce's scholarship?"

"Remember when you told me what happened at Christmas?" I nod. "And you said you felt lonely but not guilty?"

"Yes?"

Ryan continues. "Well, I hated the fact that you're lonely and I couldn't be with you. But I also saw a burden lifted. You weren't so tense anymore. You seemed happier, relaxed. I was… am so proud of you."

I bite my lip. "It wasn't just because of them. You make me happier too. Knowing you are here with me at that exact moment."

"You make me happier too," he smiles, but it is short-lived. "And no one can take that away from us." I give a small smile. "But truthfully, bumping into Joanie Jensen at the hospital and in Andreas's office, infuriated me. She reminds me so much of my step-mum, and I wanted to protect my family or myself from the likes of my dad, his wife, and their family." He leans back. "So since she wouldn't let up, I found a loophole with Bryce's scholarship."

"Okay," I respond quietly.

"You reminded us that both Kim and Bryce only have one and a half year left, and since the scholarship money have been distributed for the semester, I know that Bryce can complete this junior year without issue, which means we only have to worry about next year."

"Yeah?"

"I have told you about how my cock up of a dad continues to give me money as part of some guilt trip or another. So I've built up a nest egg with more than enough to share."

"You paid for his tuition for next year?"

He nods. "It's done. And if he needs help with college tuition, I'll make sure he gets it too."

Tears begin to form in my eyes. He's incredible. "And when you and I decide to move forward in our relationship and perhaps create mini versions of you and me, it'll be there too." His easy-going smile appears. "No pressure of course but one of these days."

My heart feels so warm right now. "But why didn't you tell me? I know you want me to have deniability…"

"You would've wanted to help and call in the cavalry," I raise my eyebrows. "You would've spoken to your sister because you have the biggest heart I know. You would've broken all the hard work of standing your ground to help.

"Isa, Bryce's story and mine have so many similarities. Raised by a hard-working single mom. Given this opportunity to attend here. Trying to show no weaknesses. And taking care of the people we love. In a way, I did this to compensate for when I was his age because I couldn't do it for my mum and me back then."

CHAPTER 38

The book *Queen Bees and Wannabes* is the inspiration for the Tina Fey-penned screenplay called *Mean Girls*. The 2004 film stars young actors, some famous at that point and some whose fame was just emerging. Ms. Fey and her composer husband, Jeff Richmond, turn it into a musical, which debuted at the Great White Way in 2018. And now, it's our school's turn to bring it to life.

For the first time in our school's history, the first public performance (for our school family - faculty, staff, and students only) is held on a Wednesday. Why? Because 'On Wednesday we wear pink,' and many of our female students want to take advantage of that fact, much to most of our male students' dismay.

On opening night that following Friday, many of the female students returned, as well as many of the local students from the other schools attended. The show for that evening sold out, and many cast, band, and crew members' families and local patrons are not given the opportunity to get tickets for that night; I contact our box office to withhold whatever tickets are not yet sold for the next two performances for that specific audience.

The early Saturday performance never has a full meet and greet as the students involved in the show need time to rest before their evening performance. However, I stay out in the lobby to greet the audience and answer questions. I thank a line of people as they exit the house, most of them are the town's elderly population as they provide their feedback, and quite a few of them have not seen the film (ha! I told Christian). Funny enough, though, many of the female audience members can relate as the show also reflects their school days.

Towards the end, a young man patiently waits for me while his young children run around. When he finally reaches me, I see it is David, my cousin Ricky's fiancee.

"Hey!" I hug him. "What are you doing here?"

"We wanted to support you, especially after the holidays," he informs me.

"Yeah… it wasn't the best day for my family. Are you by yourself?"

To answer my question, I hear two sets of pitter-patters running my way. "Tita Isa!" The twins are with them.

I crouch down to hug them. "My sweet peas!" I get the biggest hug in the world from them.

"Ooh," Ricky comes up behind the kids. "Ate, do you know the recipe for the chicken and peas dish? I think these sweet peas will be perfect for it?" He leans down and begins tickling both Charlotte and Archie.

"I don't want to be cooked and eaten!" Charlotte screams as she runs off. Several people still in the lobby gives us strange looks. Archie soon follows.

My cousin and I look at David, who is the only one still standing, and he chases after them. "Come back here, Hansel and Gretel!"

We straighten up and hug each other. "Thanks for coming."

"Well, when I heard you were doing Mean Girls, you knew I'd be here. I mean, Tina Fey pretty much based Damien off of me." He grins.

I laugh. "I absolutely would believe that if we knew Tina Fey." I watch David try to wrestle the twin back over to us. "How did you get Ate to let you take the twins?"

"Surprisingly, she and Dr. Peter," he rolls his eyes, "asked us to watch them today. Some event for Katie." He shrugs.

I frown. "And Nanay is there too, I guess."

"You know it. Tita will never miss something that's a big deal with Katie."

"Well, thank you for watching them."

"It's good practice too…" He winks.

"Hold on there. Engaged and finding a good surrogate? I am truly happy for you two!" I bring him into a giant hug.

After separating, he looks at me seriously. "Don't tell anyone yet, Ate Isa. You're the first one to know about the surrogate."

"It's not like I have anyone else to tell…"

This time his smile wavers. "I heard about what happened at Christmas."

"Yeah… well, everyone has their breaking point."

"You're a lot stronger than me. I don't know how you do it."

"I don't anymore," I sigh. "I miss those two, but I can't handle toxicity in my life. I deserve to be happy too, right?"

"Absolutely! So did I see your man in the orchestra pit?"

I feel my face reddening. "Yeah. Ryan led the band and vocals for the show."

"So you two have a little something-something going on…"

I bite my lip with a smile. "I don't kiss and tell…"

"Ate, na maan[19]," Ricky laughs.

"Walang chis mis[20], ha," I remind him. If I had to keep quiet about his growing family situation, he needs to do the same for me.

---

[19] A Filipino "come on, man"

[20] Filipino translation: Don't gossip.

CHAPTER 39

The final show and cast party (this time in Christian's dance studio) go off without a hitch. I watch as Christian leads the kids with some Tik Tok challenges and line dancing, and Ryan participates in karaoke. As for me, I feel relief after seeing that not all of my family has cut me off.

Ryan approaches me and hands me a penny. I laugh. He stands there patiently waiting for me to say something. "How am I so blessed with you?"

"You? I'm the one that feels like I'm in heaven every day I'm with you."

"Are you just trying to outdo me?"

"Just telling it as it is." He leans close when someone claps for attention. We pull away from each other and return the clap.

Scott goes to the middle of the room and does another clap set. The students and we teachers repeat. The senior does yet another one, and we follow along again.

"Dude," Jordy asks. "What's up?"

"Hey, Kacey," Scott looks at his classmate.

"What?" She responds.

"Prom?" The entire room goes silent and stares at Kacey for an answer.

"Really?" The senior girl retorts. "That's your promposal?"

"What?" Scott actually looks forlorn, and he runs up to her. "I'm serious."

"For once in your life."

"Yeah, well…"

She sighs. "Why not?"

"So yeah?" His goofy grin appears.

She laughs. "Yeah."

"Cool." He walks away, pauses, and returns to her to plant a quick kiss on the cheek. Both of them blush. Then he does walk away and turns to the rest of the audience. "What are you all staring at? Aren't we supposed to be partying?" The room then returns to its rowdy self.

However, memories of a particular prom during my student days resurface, and these recollections make my heart sink.

CHAPTER 40

Prom is one of those events that most high school student looks forward to. Even at Wellingworth, where several students of means, spend their holidays at fashion shows and shopping couture, the anticipation of participating in this tradition is contagious. Several faculty and staff members are even excited to chaperone as they can dress to the nines.

The arts department, including music and theater, is one of the two groups assigned to embrace the wardrobe and oversee the students' behavior in an off-campus location (the ballroom of a local hotel). I, for one, am not looking forward to chaperoning the event.

Living today as opposed to the past should be an easy thing to do, right? But having to face some of my biggest insecurities despite all the things I've all that I accomplished so far… well, I'm not even sure if I'll be strong enough.

The biggest hurdle I have to face is that my boyfriend, Ryan, is part of why the only prom I attended became one of the embarrassing days of my life. I don't think he even knows this; especially since he doesn't remember me during those days. And I'm too chicken to bring it up.

• • •

The prom-posals are in the full swing after the musical only two weeks before the event itself. Many of the students are pairing up if they were not dating before the event. Although endearing, it can also be a distraction during class. I, for one, request that students do not use my class time for those gestures

"What's wrong, Miss Macayo?" Willa asks. "Is everything okay?"

"I feel that class time should be focused on your work, not your social life. Plus you don't have much time left before finals," I point out.

"I still think something is wrong," Jordy adds.

"And why would that be?"

Tori Ann answers this time. "Because Mr. Marks said the same thing."

I gulp. We never discuss this; since the cast party, we haven't spent much time together. We have the occasional smile and quick hug, but nothing deeper. The honeymoon period (is that even possible when we're not married) is over. Or are we both feeling the stress? "Well, I guess that's saying we need to focus on the rest of the year during class time." The entire class groans.

• • •

Avoiding Ryan for those two weeks is too easy, and I ask myself why that is so. I tell myself it's because we had to wrap up the show that we had to prepare for the end of the year. Anything to keep me from believing that he's gotten too bored of me. Or that I am not good enough for him. Or there's something seriously wrong with me.

On the Thursday before prom, I am trudging up the stairs to my apartment. Like the last couple of days, I consider stopping by his place but change my mind at the last minute. As I turn away to climb the final set of stairs, he opens the door.

"Hey, baby."

I turn back around. He gives me a tired smile, and I return it with similar enthusiasm. "Hi!" Neither of us approaches the other, unsure if we can be closer to one another.

"Um…. about Saturday." His hand massages his neck. "We need to give focus on the students and make sure they have a good time."

I nod in agreement.

"Maybe, we should show up separately…" I wince at his idea. I guess he notices since he quickly adds, "Not that I'm going with anyone else, but I don't want us to be a distraction, you know? It's their night."

I nod again. "I concede to that."

"You make this sound like a business agreement," he ruefully comments.

"It is in a way though, isn't it? We need to act professionally, especially in these circumstances."

CHAPTER 41

I watch many upperclassmen pose for pictures and the photo booth at the lobby before taking selfies on their personal phones. Even though I have chaperoned homecoming and other school functions, I find it fascinating how the kids' actions differ but are similar to what my colleagues and I did when we were students.

The dresses are unbelievable, and I am informed that many of the ladies did their own hair and makeup, which is amazing. They all look so elegant and the young men clean up well.

I feel so old and underdressed in my very simple black dress. My hair is in an updo, thanks to Mia, who reminds me that the best way to get over this heartbreaking situation is to get dressed up and show that nothing is wrong. It's so much easier said than done.

Ryan is on the other side of the ballroom, looking ever so sexy in his classic black suit. From this distance, I feel his James Bond vibe. He catches me looking him over, and I turn my head quickly. I definitely am not ready for him, emotionally or physically.

Sebastian Fontier steps next to me. He wears a similar suit as Ryan but definitely doesn't give the same feel as him. He sneers, "So his magic has finally worn off on you?"

I sigh angrily. "If this is your way of socializing, Sebastian, you really need to work on your methods."

He sneers. "Your sister and I have never understood how frauds like him manage to infiltrate this school."

I begin seeing red. "Excuse me?"

Sebastian rolls his eyes. "Oh, Luisa, you are aware that he is not in the same pedigree as the rest of us. He is an illegitimate child; so what if the sperm donor was an ambassador? It should not have any bearing for special treatment, which I know is how he bested me."

I glare at him. "You're still on that?! You are treating him like this because of a grudge? It was nearly two decades ago, Sebastian. Get over yourself."

The science teacher squints his eyes. "Oh, are you going to imply that music, woodworking, and physical education classes should count as much as math and science courses?"

"Newsflash: I'm the theater teacher here. So yes, the arts and all the electives the kids have the option of learning, are equally as important as any of the core and language courses." I shake my head.

"And for the record, I don't care what Kool-Aid my sister is forcing you to drink, but we don't come from the same pedigree you claim to have. My parents emigrated to this country for a better life. We come from meager means," which they forget sometimes. "For someone who claims to be an intellectual scientific genius, you sure are one of the densest people. And not in a cute way like Sheldon Cooper… just an asshole."

I turn to leave, but he manhandles my wrist to prevent me from going. "You just made a terrible mistake."

Kim and Bryce waltz near us at the moment, and after a quick moment to assess the situation, the young man pushes his way between Sebastian and me, breaking the grip and letting me loose. "Are you okay, Miss Macayo?" Kim asks, her voice full of concern.

Ryan also pushes his way through a sea of students, and I catch something in his eyes that I've only seen two other times, the night of the benefit and during our talk with Kim's mom.

I run to the bathroom and shut myself in a stall. I know I'm supposed to be the adult and chaperone these kids, but this night has turned for the worse. I sink lower into my depression but no tears fell as I've used them over the course of the last few weeks.

After a few moments, I hear a gaggle of girls enter, laughing. One particular voice floats over all the rest. Zoey. Could this night continue its attack on me further?

"I cannot believe that bastard is still defending that bitch!" Her words cut through my heart. "I mean, what does he see in her anyways when he could've had a beautiful woman like me? And those two puppets of hers… thinking they're special because the boy knocked her up? I mean, that's bullshit." I hear the door open again and a new set of heels walk in. "I'm so glad I let the cat out of the bag at the benefit, thinking maybe I help his friends make a family then maybe he see how helpful I am." Wait… what did she say?

"You let people know I was pregnant? It's because of you that my mom found out and got power of attorney?" Kim's voice carries throughout the large powder room.

"It's not like you could have hidden it. I mean you're not exactly… well, me, but the baby adds another hundred pounds…."

Knowing this could instigate into something similar to what has just occurred to me, I open the door to my stall and confront all the girls. Zoey begins to laugh. "Too many losers in here." She leads her posse out, by shoving me out of the way.

I am so enraged that I may have gotten physical with her, but Kim stands next to me. "Are you okay?" I ask her. I need to be the teacher, an adult, in other words, do my job.

The young junior nods. "Are you, Miss Macayo?" I sigh. "I came in to check on you. What Mr. Fontier did was awful. Is your arm okay?" I look at my wrist, which shows the early stages of bruising.

"Oh honey," I gave her a hug her. "I know this isn't how you and Bryce were planning on for junior prom."

"Honestly, Miss Macayo, after all, you've done to help us out, we're just glad that we still got a chance to go." She gives me a small smile. "Thank you."

"Of course! I'll gladly do it again to make sure you are protected from the whole thing."

"You're going to make a great mom!" She pauses. "Mr. Marks and you will make amazing parents. I wish our scenario didn't create a rift between the two of you because I would be so upset that I had a hand in it."

"No, sweetheart, you didn't. It's…"

"Complicated, I know," she finishes for me. She heads back out to the lobby but turns around. "All I know is the way Mr. Marks looks at you is the same way Bryce looks at me. We may be young, Miss Macayo, but love is love." She goes out the door.

I look at myself in the mirror. I need to get a grip. I need… I need to talk to Ryan.

I finally leave the ladies' room, and Ryan is standing there with a very concerned look on his face. "Miss Jensen told me you were in there." I nod. "I'm glad you didn't leave. I would have run after you again."

"What?"

He puts his hands on the back of his neck. "Senior prom. Well, my senior prom. You were Steven's date, and you wore red that night, the dress you wore on Thanksgiving." I hold my breath; he remembers me from our student days. "You were absolutely breathtaking, and you still are." He gives a small smile. "But that night got so screwed up in so many ways… for both of us. Steven using you to get to Angela. Daphne using me to get to Steven. The only thing I could do to salvage it was to escort you back to your dorm. I would have hated myself if more bad things occurred to you that night.

"When we got to your residence hall, you went inside so quickly not even giving me a chance to talk to you at all. I called a few times, but Mia said that it was never a good time. I even tried asking Angela about you at graduation, only to be reminded that that was our day, not yours." He sighs, and I gulp. "Isa, I felt so horrible about that night. I am so sorry for what happened and then losing track of you after graduation, but I want you to know that I never forgot you." He reaches for my hand, which I didn't pull away from him.

I bite my lip thoughtfully. "So all this time your kindness, our relationship… was just a way to make up for that night."

He shakes his head. "No. It is because deep down I feel that in any other circumstances, we would have been closer back then too. There's something about you that I just can't describe. I'm drawn to you. I -"

"Please don't," I interrupt him, blinking my tears away. "I don't want you to say anything you'll regret later."

"Isa… " He starts and I shake my head.

"Please, don't make this harder." I slowly walk back before I purposefully head toward the exit. Once outside, I decide to walk home, just like over a decade ago.

• • •

Tonight's words keep playing over and over. Sebastian's and Angela's hatred of Ryan. Zoey's admission of being involved in the adoption. Ryan's recollection of our student days. With these revelations, my mind is on overload. I have to figure this all out.

CHAPTER 42

I wake up Sunday morning still dressed. My head is pounding, and my eyes are red. After spending the night bawling, swearing, and just getting out my frustration, my face is raw. I need food. I need… heck, I don't know what I need.

I finally turn on my phone. So many texts and a couple of voicemails from Ryan and Mia. A few messages from Angela, who rarely reaches out to me aside from the weekly Sunday dinner.

There is a pounding at the door. I close my eyes, thinking Ryan is on the other side and silently asking him to go away.

Mia's voice comes from the hallway. "Isa, please open the door! We're worried about you!"

I hesitate for a moment, not sure if I am prepared to handle anyone today.

"Come on," Mia continues knocking. She is relentless. I can already hear Old Joe complaining about the noise she is making. I sigh and slowly head to the door. I open the door and sit on the couch.

"Wow," Mia states. "Thanks for coming, Mia. I'm truly grateful, you're here, girl."

I squint my eyes. "Is that coffee?"

"Seriously, that's the first thing you ask." She hands me one of the cups. I nurse the drink. She sits on the other side of the couch, her body turned to me. "Spill."

I shake my head. "You can't keep avoiding this," my best friend says.

"Did he call me?" I ask her. She returns a confused look. "Did Ryan call for me after the prom fiasco?"

Mia sighs and takes a drink. "He did. He called every day until he left campus."

I feel the heat rising to my face. "You are my best friend since forever, and you never said jack about this to me."

Her demeanor changes slightly, like going into defense mode. "I'm sorry. I thought I was doing the right thing by protecting you."

"And when I was over the day I first saw him again? Or the day you met him? Nothing was said about it!" My voice is surprisingly even.

"I thought that whole situation had blown over, and you two were making a fresh start Obviously I was wrong. I shouldn't have listened to that piss-ant sister of yours."

"Angela?"

"She came by the room the next morning and told me that your date Steven and his best friends Colin and Ryan really did you wrong at prom and never let you be in contact with them again. I never did get the full story out of you, so I assumed her version was correct."

"And the present day?"

"As I said, I thought you two put it behind you."

I pinch the bridge of my nose. Why does it seem as if Angela did trigger this whole mess, and she's been playing innocent this whole time?

"Isa, I'm really sorry how I never told you and kept you two apart back then. I truly believed that yours was an unrequited crush and if this was a ploy to hurt you, even more, I was going to make sure he won't get the chance.

"But now, I'm second-guessing that decision. I see his compassion for the same things you enjoy and you overall. I felt so guilty but chose to stay quiet because what good would bringing up the past cause."

"Sure," I mumble.

My phone buzzes, asking to open a video conference with my mom, my sister, and her family. Mia looks at it. "It's your decision, but I truly believe your family is toxic or at least manipulative. You deserve happiness and love and to be proud of who you are without second-guessing your every decision. Blood isn't the only family you have, Isa… Wes and I love you. Your students and faculty adore you. The community cherishes you. And I know one particular neighbor of yours who loves you and is head over heels *in* love with you." She stands up. "I hope you forgive my silly way of protecting my best friend from getting hurt." She gives off a small smile. "Text or call me when you're ready or just have the itch to," She heads out the door.

The smartphone continues to alert me, but I knew that dealing with them would be a moot point. I turn it off. I will NOT resort back to feeling sorry for myself.

• • •

School is still in session. So before the students and staff ask to confirm this weekend's events, I go to the stage and grasp my surroundings. With all the talk, the exaggerated gossip… and my departure from the prom (which may have some serious consequences that I didn't previously consider), I need to prepare myself for this uphill battle.

I connect to the Bluetooth speaker and play Sarah Baralleis' "She Used to Be Mine". I look out to the empty house and belt out all of my emotions. I make it to the first chorus when the stage goes dark. What the heck? How does this even affect my Bluetooth speakers?

With a dark stage, I walk toward the wing. Darn, I wish I had left some of the glow-in-the-dark tape from the show. The lights come back on, and I sigh. But instead of *Waitress*, the opening chords from *Dear Evan Hansen* project from my speaker. I look at my phone, and it's not coming from me.

Ryan strides over to me from the other wing. I try to take off, but he gently pulls me back to the center of the stage. "You're not running away this time," he says. He looks right into my eyes and sings some of the lines from the show. His eyes never dart away from mine as he continues to sing the first verse of "Only Us."

However, as the second verse starts, I shake my head and start to sing. "I don't need more reminders of all that's been broken. I don't you to fix what I rather forget."

He holds his finger up to my lip, brushing it lightly, and continues the verse and chorus. "Clear the slate and start over… What do you say?"

His hand squeezes mine as I sing a variation of the third verse, feeling every word that comes out as if it is my story as well. "I never thought that you would actually want me… Well, that's all that I've wanted for longer than you could possibly know."

We harmonize the rest of the song together, and he pulls me to him at the end, tilting my head up until we are nose to nose. "I will never regret what I'm about to say," he whispers, eyes affix on mine. "So don't stop me and know it's true. I love you, Isa." I blink, tears forming. "And I will be by your side through everything and anything you go through. I want to be. Every moment we spend together is what I want for the rest of my life." His thumb gently wipes away the lone tear that escapes my eyes. "You are the Eliza to my Alexander. The Satine to my Christian. The Maria to my Tony. I love you." He brushes his lips onto mine, and I lean his face closer to mine to give him a more passionate kiss.

After a few minutes, when we finally pull away, I comment on the three duos he mentioned. "I love *you*, Ryan Marks, so I think we better come up with different couples to aspire to be like. Those are not the relationship goals I had in mind."

• • •

We walk into the choir room, his hand on the small of my back. The advanced choir class suddenly becomes more animated with loud whispers and hoots.

"It's about flippin' time you guys got back together!" Bryce hollers, and the rest of the kids cheers.

"So did you guys to Vegas?" Willa asks.

"Vegas, really?" One of the girls in the front row snorts.

Ryan dips his head so only I can hear. "I'm up for that if you are." I smirk.

"Or did you guys get a room during prom and just went at it?" Scott winks. The girls groan, and the guys are cheering on their male teacher.

I clap my hands once. They pipe down and repeat the clap. "We need to discuss what happened at prom."

The kids look at each other. Kim speaks up. "Well, when neither one of you returned to the dance," She looks at me with the understanding that we aren't going to talk about the incident in the ladies' room.

I turn to Ryan. He nods back up to the students.

"Mr. Fontier went on a rant about unprofessionalism and how teachers shouldn't be acting like horny teenagers," Kim finishes.

"That should be said about anyone hired to work for the school because Zoey Waines was twerking on every guys' crotch," mumbles one of the senior girls in disgust.

"Hey, she was Xavier's date, so she can grind on him however she wants," Scott pipes up. Several students begin speaking at the same time.

"But she was doing that on my date!"

"Why didn't I get some of that action?"

"I was ready to fight her."

Ryan and I look at each other. He commands the room. "Focus!" The kids quiet down. "We get that point. Is there anything non-staff-related prom affairs that we need to know about?"

"We're basically asking because rumors are always abound," I state. "I… we want to make sure that you are good kids," The students snicker, and I smirk. "For the most part, and while the staff, including ourselves, did not exhibit the best behavior, we want to make sure that you had a pleasurable evening."

"What kind of pleasure?" Ryan glares at Scott and points to the door. "Last one, I promise," The senior says flatly and defeated. "Sorry."

There is silence in the room. "It wasn't your fault, Miss M," Bryce said. "Nor yours Mr. Marks." Others offer their opinions.

"It definitely wasn't the prom we were expecting," one of the girls says. "But not everything needs to be a fairy tale."

"Except for when my wedding," another girl whispers with a soft giggle.

"No one spiked the punch…"

"Though there were people who were drunk."

"No one stripped or had sex on the dance floor."

"No one did drugs there."

"Well, there is one more incident," Tori Ann says hesitantly. We look at her. "Prom queen."

"That's right," the other kids murmur.

"But he asked for non-staff related incidents…"

Uh-oh. "What happened?" I ask.

"Well, you know how Zoey was wearing a tiara?" Kim makes me recall the confrontation in the bathroom, when I barely looked at the influencer. "I guess it was her prom queen tiara from back in the day."

"So when Camille got announced prom queen and was given a tiara, Zoey threw a fit that this year's crown was bigger than hers or something and tried to swap them," Willa adds.

"While it was on Camille's head," Jordy explains.

Wow. There is something seriously wrong with that girl. "Could she have been pissed?" Ryan ask.

"Yeah… that's why she was acting like a toddler."

"I think he means drunk," I correct the kids' line of thinking.

"Oh… I wouldn't be shocked," Scott responds. "Xavier and Zoey's whole group was drunk and high when they came in."

"And you didn't flag anyone of us to let us know?" I ask.

"Snitches get stitches," he mumbles.

"You know it takes a man to stand up to what's wrong," Ryan looks at me apologetically before returning the focus to the class. "We do appreciate you telling us now, even after the fact."

After another moment of silence, the kids begin to talk over each other about other minor scenes.

"Well, there was some shoving about stealing so-and-so's girlfriend."

"And these two girls who were yelling at each other about wearing the same dress!"

"My hair was flat before the first dance!"

"There weren't enough hors d'oeuvres."

I sigh, catch Ryan's eyes from across the room, and give a small smile. High school drama never changes, just the players in it.

CHAPTER 43

At the end of the day, Dr. Teague gathers both science and arts departments down for a meeting about the dance. Ryan escorts me to the teachers' lounge, offers me a seat before taking the chair right next to me, and puts his arm on the back of my chair. My eyes wander around the room, I notice more people in the room than the faculty. I nudge my boyfriend and nod toward the group. Ryan gives a quiet whistle when he sees the resident advisors present as well. "Wow, this is going to be the Inquisition of the 21st century."

I fidget in my seat. He squeezes my shoulder and nuzzles his face to my hair, whispering, "It's going to be all right."

"Oh get a room," a high-pitched voice passes us. Zoey saunters toward her fellow advisors. "Oh, I forgot, you already did that Saturday night instead of doing your job." She cackles.

My hand rolls up into a fist. Ryan covers them with his own hand. "I want to strangle her too, but let's see why they're here in the first place. It's possible that Andreas has something up his sleeve when it comes to her."

"But she's not entirely wrong," I whimper. "I wonder if it's a fireable offense to walk out of a volunteer assignment." He simply squeezes my hand. The grave realization is that both of our jobs could be on the line right now.

Sebastian Fontier casually walks into the room. He tries to keep a neutral face but upon seeing Ryan and me sitting together, he provides an evil smirk. It is quite unsettling.

• • •

When he sees we are mostly all present, Dr. Teague commands the room with all our focus. "I'm just going to cut to the chase. I'm disappointed with you. Many of you chose to act like the students you are supposed to be supervising, giving a bad name to this school." I look down in shame, and Ryan squeezes my hand. "And because there are multiple incidents we need to address that are very much violations of our code of conduct, I chose to meet with all of you together. If an individual incident needs to be addressed, then I will discuss that with the parties involved."

"Oh, you mean like people leaving their chaperoning job to get a hotel room to have sex?" Zoey smugly suggests, encouraging everyone to look at us. Christian shakes his head, although I'm not sure if it's because of Zoey's comment or us.

"Funny, I don't recall having a hotel room at the property or anywhere nearby," Ryan speaks up in our defense.

She snorts. "There's a lot of things you say you don't remember and break people's hearts."

My hand rolls into a fist again, and Ryan squeezes it. I close my eyes and take a deep breath. "I'll be honest with everyone." I stand up, still holding Ryan's hand. "I did leave the dance. BY MYSELF," I emphasize, looking directly at the twenty-four-year-old. "I made a mistake by not informing other teachers of my departure, and I am willing to take responsibility for my actions."

Dr. Teague doesn't respond immediately, as he's considering all the words I say and the words I'm not saying simultaneously.

Ryan also stands up. "I, too, need to apologize to you. I should've explained to my fellow chaperones that I followed I- Luisa back to our apartment complex." I snap my head up. He "escorted" me home again. "I wanted to make sure she got home safely." I felt another squeeze on my hand.

"Yeah, so they can have sex," Zoey emphasizes again.

"That's not the case." A voice comes up from the front. Christian may not stand up but he comes to our defense. "Luisa only left because she got injured during the dance." I glance briefly at Sebastian, who doesn't flinch. Ryan brushes my bruise with his thumb. "And Ryan did return but chaperoned the lobby. Many of the students or their dates rented rooms at the hotel for the night."

"You would defend them, you fa-" Zoey angrily screams.

"Zoey!" I shout before she says a derogatory word. "What the hell is your problem?!" Ryan lets go of my hand and chooses to rub my back instead. The rest of the staff stares at me in astonishment. "You are out of freaking control! You are ruining people's lives for what? Your enjoyment? Or because that's what you want? Grow the freak up already! You are an adult, get the freak over yourself." I am breathing heavily and shaking.

Ryan's other hand cups my shoulder and massages it gently. He leans over and whispers into my ear, "Baby… I'm proud of you, but you need to relax now…"

Zoey snorts. "You are an insignificant part of this school. I contribute… all you do teach theater, seriously, you can't even act." Her fellow RAs laugh.

Dr. Teague stares at her. "Miss Waines, that is quite enough."

Sebastian pipes up. "She is correct, Andreas. We work hard to make sure these students are prepared for the future, and these two," waving his hand to us, "are very inappropriate with one another, in front of the students, and teach them how to misbehave instead of becoming good citizens of the world. They do not assist the furtherance of the Wellingworth students' wellbeing, and I for one would gladly tell that to the board during their severance panel for these two."

"I disagree," Christian finally stands up. "I've had the privilege of working with both Luisa and Ryan as well as Georgette and Martin prior to them. Georgette and Martin have been having an affair for years. Going behind their spouses' backs and never addressing it. Their selfishness is often reflected in the kids' performances.

"These two have class and have a rapport with those kids that speaks volumes about their well-being. I have never seen a better group of students than those who are taught by Luisa and Ryan. And what they have," he nods at our closeness, "is pure love, and they not only show with one another but with the students and friends as well. I can only hope that I will be able to find a real love like theirs someday." He gives us a small smile and sits down. Some other people in the meeting seem to agree with his statement and also gives us a smile of support.

Dr. Teague finally responds to all of this. "Miss Macayo, Mr. Marks, I will need to speak to you privately. As well, as Mr. Fontier and Miss Waines. As for the rest of you, please know that your inability to control some of the incidents that occurred during the event will not be taken lightly. We will have a workshop that will address exactly that. You are all dismissed."

CHAPTER 44

I enter Dr. Teague's office during first period the following morning. This is one of two of my planning periods, but it also means Ryan won't be there since he has another Advanced Choir during that time. Yes, it made me nervous, but I'm pretty sure I can handle it.

Sitting down in the same sitting area I've sat in the previous three meetings I've had in this office. However, I know this time no one will be joining us (or I'm hoping no board members do).

"This has been quite the year for you," Dr. Teague starts off after he gives me a cup of coffee.

"Yes, sir. I don't think I've stopped since you requested I took over for Georgette last August."

"And you blossomed and created a theater program worthy of the Wellingworth accolades."

"Thank you, sir."

He frowns. "Unfortunately, we still need to address Saturday's incident, or in your case, multiple incidents."

My head hangs low in shame. "Yes, sir."

"I'm sure you are aware that we have security footage from the hotel." I simply nod. "We have video of Sebastian's assault on you. Do you mind if I take a look at your wrist?" I present my arm to the headmaster. The bruise is slightly fading, but the outline is still there. "You do have a right to file charges."

"No sir," I respond quickly. "I am not the type to seek out revenge or be vindictive."

"I understand," he states. "And from the rumor mill that is known as our faculty and staff, Miss Waines has been doing all she can to provoke you."

"I believe she is interested in Ryan."

The headmaster smirks. "Do you recall what I told you about Georgette prior to the job offer?"

"Yes sir."

"And Christian's revelation about her and Martin's indiscretions."

The information from last night. "Of course, sir."

"Over the years, I have been acutely aware that the positions of choir director and theater head create a bond that only the two of them can share."

"Sir?" I'm very confused.

"With the late hours of working together and having similar mindsets to create an entertaining and genuine production, the two positions are intertwined to make a partnership that can transcend beyond a professional relationship.

"This connection has proven difficult for several members of the faculty in the past and have abused it. So when the opportunity came to hire new instructors for the positions, I took a page out of Miss Tromberg's book," he chuckles. I laugh lightly as well however very confused about what he's talking about.

"As the unofficial assistant director of the program, I knew that you are the natural heir to Miss Stein's position. No one even stood a chance opposing your caliber and work ethic."

"Thank you, sir." I sip my coffee, utterly unsure of what he is getting at.

"The question remained on who will take over for Mr. Wright's vocal department that complements your vision and thought pattern and has the talent and kindness to share his gifts with the students. Thankfully Mr. Marks took me up on that offer. What I didn't anticipate is how you two were truly meant to be together."

The final words catch me off guard. "Are you saying that you set Ryan and me up?"

He laughs heartily. "I simply chose the best candidates for the jobs." My jaw drops. "Truly, Luisa, I do not run a matchmaking service or hire anyone to do so, despite what Miss Tromberg or any of the staff members think they can do in their spare time.

"I will, however, inform you that you have far succeeded your predecessor in building the theater program. Whether it is the extra strength from your relationship with Mr. Marks or just finally embracing who are truly meant to be, I have seen more growth from you over the last few months than the entirety of your student career and the last few years you've taught here combined. The board of directors is very pleased about this. That's why I can give you some latitude about Saturday's incidents.

"But to show I cannot condone your actions without consequences here is what's going to happen. You will be assisting in the move-out days in the Waines Residence Hall." My eyes widen. I'm being forced to work with Zoey? "You will be required to volunteer an extra month over the summer for some academic and more leisure camps we are hosting on-campus… I take it you are still familiar with the algebra you've taught for years.

"I will ask you and Mr. Marks to refrain from showing too much affection toward one another… when you are with the students or faculty." He pauses. "Although I am extremely grateful for your discretion around us, as many seem to flaunt their office relationship albeit a fictional one.

"And lastly, Miss Macayo, this *is* the most important one, I want you to co-lead a committee about acceptance and tolerance that we need to teach the students and staff. I think it is a critical point we need to make at this school that we are anti-discrimination. Our school's tenet about who can attend and who can succeed is a far cry from where we need to be. It may not change overnight, but I can see an improvement sooner than later.

"Do you agree to the terms?"

I process everything he says. "These are non-negotiable terms, correct?" He shakes his head. "Then I accept."

CHAPTER 45

The theater department gives a senior send-off party two days before graduation and a week before the underclassmen's finals. Kacey and the girls are all crying with overwhelming memories throughout their years here, but out of all the emotional males, Scott is the biggest surprise of them all. He is able to hold back full-blown sobs but allows the a stray tear to flow here and there. He lifts me into a bear hug, "Thanks for always believing in me, Miss M." After letting me go, he shakes hands with Ryan, who is standing next to me. "Please keep an eye on them for me, Mr. Marks."

"Isn't that something you need to ask one of the juniors to do?"

Scott looks at Bryce and Jordy with a grin. "They already know what to do. Never doubted them for a second." He leans toward the two of us. "Be careful though, I did teach them well. They'll give you hell next year." He grins.

• • •

Finals go by too fast, and move-out days arrive. Ryan and I got the same conditions, except his is the boys' dormitory, of course. I prop the main door open to assist in bringing several bigger pieces out and only allow six sets of parents at a time (two per floor) to prevent too much traffic. Around noon as I am helping one of the sophomore girls with her heavy luggage, I realize that Zoey has not been around to assist. After sending that student off, I knock at the RA apartment door, to find it unlocked. Curiously I look inside and it is completely empty.

Perplexed, I stop one of the freshmen girls, "Where is Miss Waines?"

She laughs. "She's been gone for two weeks."

"Do you know if she's okay?"

"Her? She's in Paris claiming to be some sort of Chanel influencer or something. No one believes what she says anymore."

• • •

When I get home, I do something that I haven't done in years; I go to the roof. Being so close to the school, I have a panoramic view of the campus as well as the town.

"Hey!" Mia joins me. "Brought sustenance." Pizza and Dr. Pepper.

"Where's your hubby?"

"He and Ryan are playing some sort of video game." She spreadsout a big blanket and sits down on it, putting the pizza nearby. I join her, still looking at the campus.

"It's been a hell of a year," Mia says. "Are you good with everything that's happened?"

Ryan and Wesley join us. Ryan sits and wraps his arms around me, kissing the back of my head. After Wesley tickles Mia for a bit, she hands our significant others and me a plastic cup of Dr. Pepper each, and she presents her own. "To knowing that our high school selves are at peace with who we are today…. Unequivocally happy."

We toast, and I blissfully lean back onto Ryan's chest. Being able to stand up for those you really care about makes this all the better.

EPILOGUE
10 Months Later

It's the final showing of the spring musical, *Legally Blonde*, and it's also the final time many of my students are gracing the stage. Tori Ann plays Elle Woods, and she channels Reese Witherspoon quite well. Of course, her friends are joining her on stage, with Kim playing Paulette (Bend and Snap!) and Bryce playing Kyle (aka the UPS guy). Willa portrays Vivianne and Jordy gets to manipulate both his female friends by becoming Warner.

I am preparing to dim the lights in the house when one of the freshman chorus members runs up to me. "Miss Macayo," his voice panicked. "There's an emergency backstage. We really need you back there."

"What exactly is wrong?"

"Um…" he pauses. "We can't find Elle's engagement dress."

My eyes are wide as saucers as I get the house manager's attention to take over. I speedwalk with the young man to the backstage area. I hear the opening chords of the first song, "Omigod You Guys," start up as we pass the side emergency door. We go through my studio and office to the backstage area. I ask a stage crew member if the dress has been located yet. The poor student has no idea what I am talking about. I motion to the freshman chorus member, but no one is behind me. What is happening?!

Bryce spots me. "You okay, Miss M?" He whispers when he gets close by.

"Someone said that Elle's engagement dress is missing," I reply.

"If you check with Tori Ann, she'll know where it is. She's in the changing chamber waiting for her entrance."

I quietly go over to her. On stage, the Delta Nu's are talking to a stuffed Bruiser, so I know there is not much time. I find the senior actress and whisper in the ear opposite the microphone, "Did they find the engagement dress?"

"Huh." She motions for me to step into the chamber so I can repeat the question. The dress debuts in less than a minute. It starts to spin when I have both feet on the platform. Oh no, no, no! I try to hide behind one of the "changing room curtains," but Tori Ann holds on to me. "It's almost there, but," she says her line; however instead of singing, Tori Ann turns me toward stage left.

Ryan is standing next to the "changing room." His smooth voice sings with the proper accompaniment to the show tune; his eyes glued to my shocked ones. "This verse needs to seal the deal. Now I've got to kneel and ask her to forever be by my side. Can't look like I'm desperate, but I've been waiting for it. She needs to know she's my pride." He is now on one knee, and my jaw hits the ground. My eyes are wide and full of tears as Ryan pulls a box from his pocket and opens it. An exquisite solitaire diamond ring is in the center. I bite my bottom lip, wondering if this is really happening. The next words out of his beautiful lips are spoken in the beat of the song, reassuring me that this is not a dream. "Miss Macayo, would you be my bride?"

I search his eyes and get drawn with all the passion, compassion, friendship, kindness, understanding, patience, peace, grace, hope, faith, and most of all an abundance of love emanating from those beautiful hazel orbs. Nearly 20 years ago, a fourteen-year-old me caught sight of a sixteen-year-old Ryan Marks on our old school stage, and my heart and life would never be the same again. Today, still deeply in love with him, if not more so, I agree to be forever his.

BONUS EPILOGUE
9 Months Later
Ryan's Point of View

I exhale as I attempt to perfectly tie my bow tie. I find it completely befuddling that after all these years performing in choir concerts and then becoming the choir director at Wellingworth, I'm having difficulty doing a task that I've done plenty of times. Then again, it's not every day I get married.

My beautiful Isa. I am so ashamed of myself for not realizing it was her the day I moved into my flat. I have spent many years thinking about that little sophomore, who shared the brunt of that horrendous prom incident, thanks to my supposed best mate, a pretend girlfriend, and Isa's own wretched sister. However awful that night affected both our lives, I guess I must be grateful to them for opening my eyes and heart to her.

The door opens, and Mum walks in. She is grinning as she closes the door softly. We catch each other's eyes in the mirror. "Look at you," she breathes. I turn around, and she immediately begins to work on my bow tie. "You are such a handsome man."

"You're biased," I respond, grateful for her steadier fingers.

She chuckles, "Perhaps, but I am honest." She pats the perfect tie around my neck and blinks the tears out of her eyes.

I gently brush them off her cheeks. "You know you'll always be my favorite girl, Mum."

She shakes her head with a smile. "Although I appreciate the sentiment, I truly expect you to only tell Isa and my future granddaughters that."

I grin. "Granddaughters? Are you giving me full permission to work on that tonight?"

Now she laughs fully, pointing her finger at me. "You don't get to play innocent with me."

I kiss her on the cheek. "I'll see what I can do about making sure it's granddaughters for you."

• • •

I stand nervously on the makeshift stage with headmaster Andreas Teague, who is officiating our nuptials. Colin Fairbanks, my real high school best mate, stands on my other side, supporting me as my best man. "You good?"

Nodding, I swallow my excess saliva, holding a mic in my hands. I want to surprise her by serenading my fiancé down the aisle. However, I may now regret my decision.

Andreas leans forward and whispers, "Are you ready, son?" I can only nod, saving my voice so I can give her all I have. "Good because I've been waiting for this for over two decades now." I look at him incredulously, and he winks. I hear Colin chuckling behind me.

Although both Isa and I have an affinity for musical theater, I insist the bridal party make their way down the aisle to a seasonal pop ballad, over her objections of wanting to keep it more traditional with Wagner or Pachelbel. Of course, my out-of-character persistence is a ruse. My pop rock band performs original material, but a cover is necessary for this part of the celebrations to keep up the surprise. The song choice still perfectly represents only part of my love for her. Along with my vows and the self-penned Isa-inspired songs to be performed at the reception, I can only pray that she knows that my set list is just a significantly small portion of my love and dedication to her.

I nod at my mates. Our percussionist rings bells to the opening chords to 98°'s "This Gift". I take a deep breath and begin singing. Isa's young niece, Charlotte, slowly walks down the aisle and throws mini snowflake cutouts instead of flower petals. I nod thanks to Andreas for finessing Isa's bitter sister and hard-to-deal-with mum to get the twins in the wedding party. Their stubborn pettiness prevents them from ruining Isa's and my day. Silver lining and all that.

At the chorus, several of our former students, Tori Ann, Jordy, and Willa, join my mates to be my backup singers. Upon reaching the stage, I give Charlotte a fist bump; she turns around to yell at her brother, "Come on! Stop being the tortoise!" The guests chuckle. I guess they're learning Aesop's fables at school.

Archie, Isa's nephew, carries the pillow that symbolizes our commitment and is taking his job super seriously, doing everything he can to maintain his balance. He finally reaches the platform with a toothy grin, "I'm glad she said yes." He gives me a fist bump before sticking his tongue out at his twin. I watch them as I continue to belt out the song. I can't wait to give these goofballs cousins.

Mia Devens, her best friend, is already halfway down the aisle by the time we go through the chorus the second time. I quickly glance at her husband, Wesley, who looks at her with admiration. After a brief moment with her husband, she turns her attention back to me and not-so-subtly makes a "v" shape with her fingers, pointing at her eyes before pointing them at me. I smirk.

This chorus begins to come to a close, and cousin Ricky enters with Isa by his side. I begin to shake; she is breathtaking. I am in awe of how beautiful she is in her wedding gown, a simple ivory dress that shows her off well. Her sparkling brown eyes meet mine with shock and happy tears, and I keep that contact as I sing the bridge. At this point, I'm not performing as the lyrics perfectly convey what is in my heart. "You know I'll always be true to you, and you know I'm the one you can to turn to."

As she and her cousin near, she mouths, "I love you." I swallow, forgetting the rest of the lyrics and our family and friends before grinning and mouthing the words right back, "I love you." I know there are tears of joy in my eyes, but I hold back and finally recall that I'm supposed to be singing. I try to listen to where we are in the song, but to be honest, my focus is only on Isa. Her bottom lip quivers as she finally stops biting the inside of it.

    When she reaches me, her tearful eyes are filled with passion as she helps me with the lyrics by singing, "It's something to last for as long as we live." I reach for her hand, lacing our fingers together. Our eyes are only on each other. I'm drinking her in, body and soul, and I feel she's doing the same to me. I've known that I've always been drawn to her and that feeling is a constant since we first shared the stage as students. I will always remind her that I'm here for her and support her through everything we go through.

    In perfect harmony with my voice shaking with happiness and anticipation and her smile that lights up this whole room, we sing the final line together as a promise, "Tonight I'm gonna give you all my heart can give."

ADDITIONAL RESOURCES

Check out the "Real Me Because of You" concept boards, the playlists, memes and "live" texts from the book:

www.creativereflectionsmedia.com/blog/realme

ACKNOWLEDGEMENTS

I want to thank my Lord and Savior for giving me the opportunity to share this story. I am grateful for the support from my husband, my son, my parents, my sister and my extended family (both relatives and close friends). My daughter whose love of rom-coms encouraged me to put my ideas on paper. One of my best friends and my beta reader, Cecily, whose love of books helped me keep going through the times I have writers' block. Thank you to Veronica, who met me while I was a substitute teacher in her Algebra 1 class, for creating a perfect visual of Isa and Ryan. Jennifer Johnson-Garcia for giving me the courage to offer this to the public. And to you for taking a chance on my writing. I pray you enjoy it.

ART CREDITS

Cover

Art by Veronica Jimenez

Illustrations

Text Messages by TextingStory.com

Notebook Paper Texture by

Songs

"Helpless"
Hamilton
Written by Lin-Manuel Miranda

"Hand in My Pocket"
Jagged Little Pill
Written by Alanis Morrisette, Glen Ballard

"People Will Say We're In Love"
Oklahoma!
Written by Oscar Hammerstein II, Richard Rodgers

"Star Spangled Banner"

Written by Francis Scott Key

"See Her Smile"
tick, tick… BOOM!
Written by Jonathan Larson

"On an Evening in Roma (Sott'er Celo de Roma)" Written by Alessandro Taccani, Nan Frederics, Umberto Bertini

"She Used to Be Mine"
Waitress
Written by Sara Bareilles

"Only Us"
Dear Evan Hansen
Written by Benj Pasek and Justin Paul

"Omigod You Guys"
Legally Blonde
Written by Neil Benjamin and Laurence O'Keefe

"This Gift"
Written by Anders Bagge, Amthor Birgisson, Dane Deviller, Sean Hosein

ABOUT THE AUTHOR

MJ Apple is a pen name. The writer and her husband have two teenage children and two puppies and raised them in various part of the US, most recently in the South. She currently teaches high school math and officiates swim meets. She advocates her children and students to embrace their talented passions of performing and visual arts and continuing to grow in their faith.

Follow her on social media: @authormjapple

| Instagram | Facebook | Tik Tok |

Made in the USA
Columbia, SC
30 January 2023

9782bb90-2f7d-4660-a1de-1abab584faf6R02